Immortal Love. Four Ethereal Ghostly, Vampire and Werewolf Romantic Love Stories

People with Books

Published by People with Books, 2023.

This is a work of fiction. Similarities to real people, places, or events are entirely coincidental.

IMMORTAL LOVE. FOUR ETHEREAL GHOSTLY, VAMPIRE AND WEREWOLF ROMANTIC LOVE STORIES

First edition. September 16, 2023.

ISBN: 979-8223562405

Written by People with Books.

Also by People with Books

How To Handle A Marriage Breakup Volume 1 of 3
How To Handle a Marriage Breakup Volume 2 of 3
How To Handle a Marriage Breakup Volume 3 of 3
Positive Talk, Happy Home Strategies for Effective Communication with Children
What the F*ck Do I do Now? The Stress Solution: Effective Techniques for a Peaceful Mind
50 Bedtime Adventure Stories for Young Kids Book 1
50 Bedtime Adventure Stories for Young Kids Book 2
50 Young Kids Learning to Share Bedtime Stories Book 1
50 Young Kids Learning to Share Bedtime Stories Book 2
Unconditional Love: A Parent's Guide to Raising Special Needs Children
The Beginner's Complete Ketogenic Diet Cookbook With 3 Months of Weekly Diet Plans Including Recipes
Guide to Anger Management With Kids: A Parent's Guide to Raising Emotionally Balanced Children
Help me Mommy. OCD Help. Understanding OCD in Children: A Guide for Parents
My Life is so F*cked Up:Understanding Anxiety: Exploring its Causes, Symptoms, and Treatment Options
The Complete Handbook for Managing Depression and Anxiety as an Adult
The Ultimate Italian Cookbook: A Selection of the Best Italian Traditional Recipes for Every Kitchen
Haunted by a Ghostly Love
The Art of Making Friends: Unlocking the Secrets of College Social Life
The Art of Self Management. Practical Strategies and Insights to Take Control of Your Life and Achieve Personal and Professional Success.
The Power of Positive Thinking: Unlocking Your Success Potential
Unlocking Financial Freedom Harnessing the Power of Feng Shui
50 Fun at School Kids Stories Book 1. Back to School Stories for Kids
Unlocking Your Potential: Mastering Self-Discipline, Self-Control, and Mental Strength for Goal Achievement
The Keto Cookbook for Women: Delicious Recipes for Rapid Weight Loss
The Keto Family Cookbook: Delicious Low-Carb Recipes for the Whole Family

Oliver's 50 Bedtime Stories for Young Boys Book 1.
Oliver's 50 Bedtime Stories for Young Boys Book 2
Immortal Love. Four Ethereal Ghostly, Vampire and Werewolf Romantic Love Stories

Table of Contents

Immortal Love. Four Ethereal Ghostly, Vampire and Werewolf Romantic Love Stories

Introduction:

Dive into the seductive shadows of the supernatural with "Immortal Love: Four Ethereal Ghostly, Vampire, and Werewolf Romantic Love Stories." These four tantalizing tales will ignite your imagination, quicken your pulse, and leave you yearning for more.

In the realm of the ethereal, love takes on a life of its own, defying the boundaries of mortality. Ghostly lovers whisper their eternal devotion, vampires navigate the thrilling dance between immortality and human desire, and powerful werewolves find their hearts entwined with those of mortals.

1. Eternal Embrace: A Vampire Romance: In the shadowy world where immortality and desire collide, "Eternal Embrace: A Vampire Romance" beckons you to surrender to a love that defies time and temptation. This intoxicating tale immerses you in the thrilling, forbidden romance between a vampire with an ancient past and a mortal with a secret that could change their destiny forever. Prepare to be enraptured by the allure of eternal love, where passion knows no bounds, and danger lurks in every enticing embrace.

2. Prepare to be captivated by "Cursed Hearts: A Romance in the Haunted Mansion," a spellbinding tale of love and mystery that unfolds within the chilling confines of an eerie mansion. As forbidden secrets and ghostly apparitions intertwine, two hearts find themselves drawn together by a force that defies the boundaries of the living and the dead. In the shadows of this haunting love story, unearth the secrets of a mansion with a cursed past, where love and the supernatural converge in a tale of longing and redemption.

3. Step into the moonlit world of "Ensnared by the Werewolf's Heart: A Love in the Night," where passion ignites beneath the stars and danger prowls in the darkness. This mesmerizing romance unravels the tale of an unlikely love between a mortal and a fierce werewolf, their destinies intertwined by a force more powerful than they could have imagined. As they navigate the treacherous terrain of love and the supernatural, secrets are revealed, hearts are tested, and a love story unfolds that will leave you enchanted and entranced.

4."Love from the Other Side: An Astral Projection Romance" invites you to explore the extraordinary realms of love and connection beyond the boundaries of the physical world. In this mesmerizing tale, two souls find themselves drawn together through the mystical art of astral projection, discovering a love that transcends the constraints of time and distance. As they navigate the ethereal plane, they embark on a passionate and otherworldly romance that will leave you spellbound, proving that true love can bridge even the most profound cosmic divides. Immerse yourself in a love story that defies the ordinary and unfolds in the luminous embrace of the astral realm.

PEOPLE WITH BOOKS

"Immortal Love" invites you to embrace the otherworldly, where love transcends time, death, and the boundaries of reality. Each story is a captivating journey into a world where ethereal beings collide with passionate humans, igniting a whirlwind of desire and destiny.

If you crave stories that pulse with forbidden love, where the supernatural and the romantic coalesce in a symphony of desire, then "Immortal Love" will enchant you. Join us on this exhilarating journey where love is eternal, passion is unbridled, and the ethereal and erotic merge in four spellbinding tales. Unleash your desires and experience the allure of "Immortal Love" today.

BOOK 1: Eternal Embrace: A Vampire Romance

BOOK 2: Cursed Hearts: A Romance in the Haunted Mansion

BOOK 3: Moonlit Encounter Ensnared by the Werewolf's Heart

BOOK 4: Love From The Other Side: An astral Projection Romance

Chapter 1: Eternal Embrace: A Vampire Romance: The Mysterious Stranger

Elena Rousseau, a woman of quiet grace and hidden desires, had always found solace in the unassuming beauty of Wraithhaven. It was a place where time seemed to stand still, where cobblestone streets whispered tales of yesteryears, and where the ancient oaks cradled the town's most enigmatic secrets.

On the cusp of her twenty-ninth birthday, Elena's auburn hair flowed like liquid flame, cascading down her back in a fiery cascade of unruly curls. Her emerald-green eyes held wisdom beyond her years, a reflection of a life spent immersed in the pages of books that lined the shelves of Pages & Prose, Wraithhaven's cherished bookstore.

Elena's existence followed the tranquil rhythm of routine—a morning walk through the town square, where sunlight painted the facades of historic buildings in hues of gold; her days spent tending to the silent companions that lined the shelves, their stories echoing in the hush of paper and ink; and evenings that unfurled like the petals of a nocturnal blossom, with a cup of chamomile tea and the whispered secrets of the latest novel.

She was content in her solitude, having chosen to remain in Wraithhaven while her family ventured into the bustling heart of the city. The town, with its secrets and gentle embrace, had become her home, her sanctuary.

But on this particular night, a peculiar unease hung in the air, like an unresolved melody that lingered after the music had ceased. The moon, heavy and full, cast long shadows that danced across the cobblestone streets. Elena's steps quickened, her heart's rhythm echoing the rapid clip of her boots on the stone.

Her path led her to a narrow alleyway, a shortcut she'd traversed countless times before. Yet tonight, the alleyway seemed cloaked in an inexplicable darkness, as if it were harboring secrets it had never revealed before. An involuntary shiver cascaded down her spine.

She dismissed her unease as the whims of a capricious imagination, attributing it to the eerie enchantment that often descended upon Wraithhaven when the sun dipped below the horizon.

And then, she heard it—a whisper, softer than a breath, silkier than a sigh. The voice seemed to emanate from the very heart of the darkness, a siren's call that beckoned her forward.

Elena's heart skipped a beat. She hesitated, her senses attuned to the faintest of movements, her ears straining for any sound in the stillness of the night.

"Is someone there?" she called out, her voice trembling in the velvety silence.

For a heartbeat, there was nothing but the moon's silvery glow, casting eerie patterns on the alley's cobbled floor. And then, as though summoned by her words, a figure emerged—a man, tall and enigmatic, his dark silhouette framed by the moon's ethereal light.

His hair, like a raven's wing, was tousled as if tousled by the night's fingers, and his eyes—oh, his eyes—a deep, mesmerizing shade of amethyst, sparkled with a mystery that seemed to draw her in.

In his presence, the world seemed to pause, the very essence of time slowing to savor this ephemeral moment. Elena's breath caught in her throat, her heart's rhythm quickening like a galloping stallion.

A half-smile tugged at the corner of his lips, revealing a hint of pearl-white teeth. His voice, when it finally came, was a melodious symphony of darkness and allure.

"You shouldn't be here alone, my dear," he murmured, his words like a gentle caress, his presence like an enchantment that defied the ordinary. "The night can be a treacherous place."

Elena's emerald eyes, wide with a potent mix of fear and fascination, locked onto his enigmatic gaze. In that stolen moment, beneath the watchful eye of the moon, Elena Rousseau's life shifted irrevocably. It was a moment of beginnings and secrets, of a mysterious stranger who would come to embody both danger and desire.

Little did she know that this enigmatic figure, this stranger whose name was yet unknown, was the catalyst for a journey that would explore the depths of love, the allure of the unknown, and the unfathomable mysteries of the heart.

Chapter 2: Forbidden Desires

In the wake of that moonlit encounter with the enigmatic stranger who had introduced himself as Adrian, Elena's world was irrevocably altered. Each night, she found herself gazing at the silvery orb in the night sky, wondering if he would return if their paths would cross once more. And each day, she went about her routines with a lingering sense of anticipation, a yearning that refused to be extinguished.

Elena's life had always been one of predictability and order, the very essence of stability. But now, a wild tempest of emotions raged within her—a tempest named Adrian. His voice, his touch, and the allure of his amethyst eyes haunted her waking thoughts and invaded her dreams.

As the weeks passed, Elena couldn't deny the magnetic pull she felt toward the enigmatic vampire. She longed to see him again, to unravel the mysteries that shrouded his existence. Yet, she also grappled with an innate fear, a primal instinct that whispered warnings of the danger he posed.

One evening, as the sun dipped below the horizon, painting the sky in fiery hues, Elena found herself drawn to the alleyway where their paths had first crossed. She couldn't explain the compulsion that had taken hold of her, only that it felt as inexorable as the tide.

The alley was cloaked in shadow, its cobbled stones cool beneath her feet. She hesitated at the entrance, her heart pounding in her chest. The alley seemed to hold its breath, as if it, too, awaited his arrival.

And then, from the depths of the darkness, he emerged—an apparition of the night, his presence as intoxicating as the finest of wines. His amethyst eyes met hers, and she felt a shiver of longing cascade down her spine.

"Adrian," she breathed, his name a sigh on her lips.

He smiled a rueful expression that held both desire and restraint. "Elena," he replied, his voice a velvety caress. "You shouldn't be here."

The words should have been a warning, a reminder of the dangers that lurked in the shadows. But Elena couldn't tear her gaze away from him, couldn't resist the pull that drew her closer.

"Why did you come back?" she asked, her voice barely above a whisper.

Adrian stepped closer, the moonlight catching the raven-black waves of his hair. "I couldn't stay away," he confessed, his eyes holding a vulnerability that both surprised and captivated her. "There's something about you, Elena. Something I can't resist."

As his hand brushed against hers, a current of electricity surged between them—a tangible, undeniable connection that left them breathless. Elena felt herself drawn into his embrace, her desires warring with her fears.

Their lips met in a kiss that ignited a passion as fierce as the sun, a forbidden desire that burned brighter in the shadows of the night. In that stolen moment, Elena knew that her fate was sealed, her heart irrevocably entwined with the enigmatic vampire who had awakened a hunger within her—a hunger for love, for danger, and for the forbidden desires that would define their tumultuous journey.

Little did Elena know that this stolen kiss was but the beginning of a love story that would unravel the very fabric of time, a tale of longing, sacrifice, and the undeniable allure of a love that defied all reason.

Chapter 3: A Dark Secret

In the wake of their stolen kiss in the moonlit alley, Elena found herself ensnared in a web of emotions she had never known before. Adrian, the enigmatic vampire, had become an undeniable presence in her life, a haunting melody that played in the background of her every thought.

Days turned into weeks, and their clandestine encounters continued, each one deepening the connection between them. Elena couldn't help but be drawn to the enigmatic allure of Adrian—the way his amethyst eyes held secrets untold, the way his touch sent shivers down her spine, and the way his lips tasted of both danger and desire.

But as their love grew, so did Elena's curiosity. She yearned to understand the man who had entered her life like a tempest, to peel back the layers of mystery that shrouded his existence. And so, one fateful night, as they sat together on a secluded bench in the town square, bathed in the soft glow of the moon, Elena summoned the courage to ask the question that had weighed on her heart.

"Adrian," she began, her voice a gentle caress, "there's so much I don't know about you. About your past, your origins..."

Adrian's gaze, which had been fixed on the distant horizon, shifted to meet hers. In the depths of his amethyst eyes, she glimpsed a shadow—a hint of sadness that tugged at her heart.

"There are things about me, Elena," he admitted, his voice tinged with both reluctance and sorrow, "that I can never fully share."

Elena felt a pang of frustration and longing. She had sensed from the beginning that Adrian carried a heavy burden, that his past was a labyrinth of secrets and regrets. But she had hoped that their love would break down the walls he had erected.

"Please, Adrian," she implored, reaching out to touch his hand, "I want to know you. All of you."

For a moment, he seemed torn, as if battling an inner turmoil. And then, with a sigh that held the weight of centuries, he began to speak.

"My life, Elena," he confessed, "is not like yours. I am not like you. I am a creature of the night, bound by darkness and desire. My existence is a tapestry woven with blood and secrets."

As Adrian's story unfolded, Elena listened in rapt attention, her heart heavy with empathy. He spoke of a life that spanned centuries, of the sacrifices he had made to survive, and of the constant struggle to resist the primal urges that
defined his kind.

But there was one secret he couldn't bring himself to reveal—a truth so dark, so forbidden, that it remained locked away in the deepest recesses of his soul.

As their night together drew to a close, Elena couldn't help but feel a mixture of emotions—compassion for the man she had come to love, a longing to unravel the mysteries of his existence, and a growing awareness of the danger that lurked in the shadows.

Little did she know that Adrian's dark secret was but the tip of the iceberg, that their love would be tested in ways she could never have imagined, and that the forbidden desires that bound them would lead them down a treacherous path—one fraught with challenges, sacrifices, and a love that would be tested to the limits of eternity.

Chapter 4: The Bond Deepens

As the days turned into weeks and the weeks into months, Elena's connection with Adrian, the enigmatic vampire, deepened. Their love was like an intoxicating elixir, a force that defied reason and defied the boundaries of human and vampire.

Elena's life had become a mesmerizing dance—a dance of stolen kisses beneath the moonlight, whispered promises in the shadows, and a hunger that could only be satiated by each other's presence. Together, they had forged a bond that was both forbidden and unbreakable.

One warm summer evening, as fireflies painted the night with their ethereal glow, Elena and Adrian found themselves beneath the ancient oak tree in the heart of Wraithhaven. Its gnarled branches stretched toward the heavens like the fingers of an ancient sentinel, and its roots delved deep into the earth as if drawing strength from the very core of the world.

They sat side by side on a weathered bench, their fingers entwined. The moon hung low in the sky, casting a silver sheen upon their faces. Elena leaned against Adrian's shoulder, her heart swelling with a love that transcended the boundaries of time and mortality.

"Adrian," she whispered, her voice a tender caress, "I never thought I could feel this way. I never imagined that love could be so powerful, so all-consuming."

Adrian's amethyst eyes gazed into hers, filled with a mixture of adoration and longing. "Elena," he replied, his voice a velvety murmur, "our love is a force of nature, a fire that burns brighter with each passing moment. I've never known a love like this."

Their lips met in a kiss that held the promise of forever, a kiss that sealed their hearts together in an unbreakable bond. In that stolen moment beneath the ancient oak, amidst the symphony of nature's night, Elena and Adrian's love deepened, their desires merging into a passion that knew no bounds.

But as their love flourished, so did the challenges they faced. The vampire society, with its strict rules and traditions, cast a shadow over their happiness. Some viewed their love as an abomination, a breach of the sacred laws that governed their kind.

Elena and Adrian found themselves entangled in a web of intrigue and danger, as rival vampires sought to tear them apart. Their love became a beacon of hope and defiance, a testament to the power of love to conquer even the darkest of forces.

Amid adversity, Elena and Adrian's bond deepened further, their love proving to be an unyielding force that defied all odds. Together, they would face the challenges that lay ahead, drawing strength from each other and the love that had become their guiding light.

Little did they know that their love story was far from over, that the trials they would face would test the limits of their devotion, and that the depths of their passion would lead them on a journey that would span the ages—a journey of love, sacrifice, and the enduring power of an immortal bond.

Chapter 5: The Vampire Society

Elena's love for Adrian had thrust her into a world she had never imagined—a world of ancient traditions, complex hierarchies, and a society hidden in the shadows. Adrian, the enigmatic vampire who had captured her heart, was not just a solitary creature of the night; he was part of a larger vampire community, a society that spanned the ages.

As Elena delved deeper into this clandestine world, she began to understand the intricacies and complexities of vampire society. It was a society that had evolved over centuries, with its own rules, customs, and rituals. Beneath the veneer of normalcy, vampires lived by a code that governed their interactions, their relationships, and their very existence.

Adrian, being an elder vampire, held a position of prominence within this society. He was respected and feared, his influence extending over a network of vampires that stretched far and wide. He had been part of this world for centuries, and his knowledge of its intricacies was vast.

Elena, on the other hand, was an outsider—a human who had been initiated into this hidden society through her love for Adrian. She learned about the Council of Elders, the governing body that enforced the laws of the vampire world, and the delicate balance of power that existed among the vampire clans.

But she also discovered the darker aspects of vampire society—the rivalries, the betrayals, and the constant struggle for dominance. Some viewed her relationship with Adrian as a threat, a challenge to the established order, and they would stop at nothing to see their love torn asunder.

As Elena navigated the treacherous waters of vampire society, she clung to the love that had brought her into this world. She and Adrian faced challenges that tested the strength of their bond, as they fought to protect their love from those who sought to extinguish it.

But amidst the complexities and dangers of vampire society, Elena also found moments of beauty and wonder. She witnessed ancient rituals, attended lavish gatherings, and explored the hidden corners of a world that existed in parallel to the human realm. She saw the depths of Adrian's love and the sacrifices he had made to protect her.

Their love story became a beacon of hope within the vampire society, a symbol of the possibility of love transcending boundaries. It was a love that defied the rules, challenged the norms, and dared to exist in the face of adversity.

As Elena and Adrian navigated the intricacies of this hidden world, they were drawn closer together, their love becoming an unbreakable bond that defied the constraints of time and society. Together, they would face the challenges that lay ahead, determined to protect their love and defy the forces that sought to tear them apart.

Little did they know that their journey through vampire society was far from over, that their love would be tested in ways they could never have imagined, and that the true depths of their passion would be revealed in the face of adversity.

Chapter 6: Love and Danger

As Elena and Adrian's love deepened amidst the complexities of vampire society, they found themselves entangled in a perilous dance—one where love and danger were inseparable partners. Their relationship had become a beacon of hope and defiance within the secretive world of vampires, but it had also made them targets of jealousy and intrigue.

The Council of Elders, the governing body of the vampire society, viewed their love with suspicion. Adrian's position as an elder vampire had given him influence and power, but it also made him a threat to those who sought to maintain the status quo. The Council's strict rules and traditions clashed with the unorthodox love between a vampire and a human.

Elena, though not bound by the same rules as vampires, found herself navigating a world filled with intrigue and danger. Her love for Adrian had made her a target, and she soon realized that her life was in constant peril. Some vampires saw her as a weakness, a vulnerability that could be exploited to bring down Adrian.

One evening, as they sought solace in each other's arms beneath the moonlit sky, they were ambushed by a group of rival vampires. The attackers, driven by jealousy and a thirst for power, sought to use Elena as leverage against Adrian.

Elena's heart pounded in her chest as the vampires closed in, their eyes glinting with malice. Adrian's protective instincts kicked in, and he fought fiercely to defend the woman he loved. The battle that ensued was a whirlwind of fangs and claws, a deadly dance in which the outcome was uncertain.

Amid the chaos, Elena's life hung in the balance, her very existence a bargaining chip in the power struggle within vampire society. She watched in horror as the attackers threatened to harm her, their cold, unyielding gazes sending shivers down her spine.

But Adrian's love for Elena was a force that could not be underestimated. With a surge of strength born of desperation and love, he overcame his assailants, driving them away with a ferocity that left no doubt of his determination to protect the woman he cherished.

Elena clung to Adrian, her heart pounding, her breaths coming in ragged gasps. The danger had passed, but the threat against their love remained. It was a stark reminder of the perilous path they had chosen—a path where love and danger were intertwined, where the very act of loving each other made them vulnerable.

In the aftermath of the attack, Elena and Adrian found solace in each other's arms. Their love had been tested, and it had emerged stronger than ever. They knew that the challenges they faced were far from over and that the dangers of vampire society still loomed on the horizon.

But as they held each other beneath the moon's gentle gaze, they also knew that their love was worth the risks, that it was a force that could conquer even the darkest of adversaries. Together, they would face whatever dangers lay ahead, determined to protect their love and defy the forces that sought to tear them apart.

Little did they know that their love story would become a legend in the annals of vampire society, a tale of love and danger that would be told for centuries to come—a testament to the enduring power of love to conquer all obstacles, even in the face of the deadliest of foes.

Chapter 7: A Rivalry Ignites

In the wake of the ambush that had tested their love and left them shaken, Elena and Adrian's relationship faced a new challenge—one that would ignite a fierce rivalry within the vampire society and threaten to tear them apart.

Word of the attack had spread like wildfire among the vampires, and it had not gone unnoticed by the Council of Elders. The Council viewed Elena as a dangerous element, a human who had become entwined in the affairs of their kind. They believed her presence was a threat to the secrecy and stability of the vampire world.

Amidst the whispers and conspiracies that swirled within vampire society, a rival faction emerged—a group of vampires who sought to use Elena as a pawn in their quest for power. Led by a charismatic and cunning vampire named Lucius, this faction believed that if they could control Elena, they could control Adrian and manipulate the balance of power within the Council.

Lucius, with his piercing gaze and silver tongue, saw Elena as a means to an end—a way to undermine Adrian's influence and rise to prominence within the vampire hierarchy. He had long harbored ambitions of supplanting Adrian as an elder, and Elena's presence provided him with the leverage he needed.

Elena and Adrian were thrust into a perilous game of cat and mouse, as Lucius and his followers plotted to capture and control Elena. Their love became a battleground, a symbol of defiance against those who sought to manipulate their destiny.

One fateful night, as Elena and Adrian sought refuge in a remote cabin nestled deep in the woods, Lucius and his followers closed in. They launched a coordinated attack, their powers and cunning tactics putting Elena and Adrian's lives in grave danger.

The cabin became a battleground, with spells and supernatural abilities clashing in a flurry of violence and chaos. Elena and Adrian fought side by side, their love a source of strength in the face of adversity. But Lucius was a formidable adversary, and his determination to control Elena was unwavering.

As the battle raged on, Elena's life hung in the balance once more. She knew that if Lucius succeeded in capturing her, their love would be torn asunder, and the delicate balance of vampire society would be upended.

In a final, desperate confrontation, Adrian and Lucius faced off, their powers colliding in a spectacular display of supernatural energy. It was a battle that would determine the fate of their love and the future of vampire society.

As the dust settled and the echoes of their conflict faded, Elena and Adrian stood victorious. Lucius and his followers had been defeated, their ambitions thwarted. But the danger had not passed entirely, and the rivalry within vampire society had only grown more intense.

Elena and Adrian's love had been tested once again, and it had emerged stronger than ever. They knew that the challenges they faced were far from over and that the rivalry ignited by their love would continue to burn. But they also knew that their love was a force that could not be extinguished, a love that defied all odds and would endure through the ages.

In the aftermath of the battle, as they held each other in the moon's soft glow, Elena and Adrian were determined to face whatever challenges lay ahead. Their love was a flame that would burn eternally, a beacon of hope and defiance in a world where love and danger were inseparable.

Little did they know that their love story was far from reaching its conclusion, that the rivalry ignited by their love would lead to even greater trials, and that the depths of their passion would be revealed in the face of adversity.

Chapter 8: Bloodlust and Temptation

The aftermath of the battle with Lucius and his followers left Elena and Adrian with a newfound awareness of the dangers that surrounded them. The rivalry within vampire society had ignited with an intensity that threatened to consume them, and the struggle to protect their love had never been more precarious.

As the days turned into nights, Elena and Adrian's relationship faced a relentless onslaught of challenges. The thirst for power and control within vampire society had reached a fevered pitch, and Elena's presence remained a divisive force among the vampires.

Adrian's position as an elder vampire made him a prime target for those who sought to unseat him and claim his power. They believed that by controlling Elena, they could manipulate Adrian and bend him to their will. The temptations of power and influence were ever-present, and Adrian's loyalty to Elena was constantly tested.

Elena, too, found herself grappling with new temptations. The allure of immortality and the promise of eternal life beckoned her from the shadows. The dark desires of the vampire world were a constant temptation, and Elena struggled to resist their seductive pull.

One evening, as they wandered through the moonlit streets of Wraithhaven, their love became a sanctuary in a world filled with bloodlust and temptation. They held each other close, their hearts entwined in an unbreakable bond.

"Elena," Adrian murmured, his voice a caress against her ear, "the temptations of our world are relentless. The thirst for power, the lure of immortality—they are ever-present."

Elena nodded, her emerald eyes filled with understanding. "I know, Adrian. But our love is stronger than any temptation. It's what sets us apart."

Their love was a testament to the enduring power of the heart, a love that defied the darkest of desires and the most seductive of temptations. As they clung to each other beneath the watchful gaze of the moon, they knew that their love was worth the sacrifices they would make, and the challenges they would face.

But the rivalry within vampire society showed no signs of abating. Lucius and his followers, though defeated, continued to plot and scheme, determined to gain the upper hand. The Council of Elders watched their every move, their suspicion of Elena growing with each passing day.

In the face of these challenges, Elena and Adrian's love burned brighter than ever. It was a love that defied the odds, a love that had withstood the tests of time and adversity. Together, they were determined to protect their love and defy the forces that sought to tear them apart.

As they ventured into the unknown, their love remained a beacon of hope and defiance, a flame that would continue to burn in a world where bloodlust and temptation were ever-present. Little did they know that their journey was far from over, that the true depths of their love and commitment would be revealed in the face of the greatest of challenges.

Chapter 9: The Cursed Kiss

Elena and Adrian's love had weathered countless storms, but a new and sinister threat loomed on the horizon—one that would test the very foundations of their relationship and challenge the limits of their devotion.

As tensions within vampire society continued to escalate, rumors of a legendary artifact known as the "Cursed Kiss" began to surface. It was said to be an ancient talisman with the power to bind the souls of two lovers in an unbreakable union but at a terrible cost.

The Cursed Kiss was believed to have been lost to the ages, its existence dismissed as mere legend. However, as whispers of its reemergence grew louder, a new wave of intrigue and danger swept through the vampire world.

Lucius, undeterred by his previous failures, saw the Cursed Kiss as the ultimate weapon to use against Elena and Adrian. If he could obtain the artifact, he believed he could control their love, manipulate their destiny, and secure his position as an elder vampire.

Elena and Adrian, aware of the threat that the Cursed Kiss posed, embarked on a perilous quest to find the artifact before it could fall into the wrong hands. They journeyed through ancient crypts, consulted with ancient vampire sages, and followed cryptic clues that led them deeper into the heart of vampire lore.

Their search took them to the far corners of the vampire world, and with each step, their love was tested in ways they could never have imagined. The temptations of power and control, the lure of the Cursed Kiss itself, threatened to tear them apart.

One fateful night, they found themselves in the shadowy depths of a forgotten vampire sanctuary—a place of dark rituals and ancient secrets. It was there that they uncovered the truth about the Cursed Kiss and the terrible price it demanded.

The artifact could indeed bind their souls in an unbreakable union, but it came at a cost—the sacrifice of one of their mortal lives. To obtain the power of the Cursed Kiss, one of them would have to relinquish their humanity, becoming a vampire for all eternity.

Elena and Adrian stood before the artifact, their hearts heavy with the weight of the choice that lay before them. To bind their love in a way that transcended time and mortality was a temptation beyond measure, but the price was a steep one.

In that pivotal moment, as they gazed into each other's eyes, they knew that their love was worth any sacrifice. It was a love that had defied the odds, conquered the darkest of challenges, and burned brighter than any temptation or danger.

With a shared determination, they made their choice—a choice that would bind their souls together in an unbreakable union, a choice that would forever alter the course of their love story.

As their lips met in a kiss that sealed their fate, the world seemed to hold its breath. The Cursed Kiss had been
activated, and their love was now bound by a power that transcended time and space.

But the consequences of their choice remained uncertain, and the challenges that lay ahead were greater than any they had faced before. Their love story had taken a new and unpredictable turn, one that would test the very essence of their love and commitment.

Little did they know that the Cursed Kiss held secrets of its own and that their journey was far from reaching its conclusion. The true nature of their love and the depths of their devotion would be revealed in the face of the ultimate challenge.

Chapter 10: Immortal Love

The power of the Cursed Kiss had bound Elena and Adrian's souls together in an unbreakable union, but it had come at a great cost—the sacrifice of Elena's mortal life. She had become a vampire, destined to walk the immortal path alongside Adrian for all eternity.

The transformation had not been without its challenges. Elena had to adapt to her newfound vampiric nature—her heightened senses, her insatiable thirst for blood, and the limitations of her existence. It was a journey of self-discovery and adaptation, and Adrian was her guiding light in the darkness of her new existence.

Their love had transcended the boundaries of time and mortality, becoming an immortal flame that burned brighter with each passing night. Together, they embarked on a new chapter of their love story, one that defied the constraints of age and the limitations of humanity.

As the centuries passed, Elena and Adrian's love deepened, evolving into a bond that was both timeless and unbreakable. They witnessed the ebb and flow of human history, the rise and fall of empires, and the changing landscapes of the world.

Their love story became a legend among vampires, a tale of a love that had conquered all obstacles and withstood the test of time. It was a story of sacrifice and devotion, of two souls bound together in an eternal union.

But even as they reveled in their immortal love, challenges continued to emerge. The rivalry within vampire society persisted, and new threats to their happiness arose. They faced enemies from their past, as well as new adversaries who sought to test the limits of their love.

Through it all, Elena and Adrian remained steadfast in their commitment to each other. Their love was a beacon of hope and defiance, a testament to the enduring power of the heart. It was a love that had faced the darkest of challenges and emerged stronger with each trial.

As they stood together beneath the moon's gentle glow, their hands entwined, they knew that their journey was far from over. Their love had become an immortal legend, a story that would be told for generations to come. It was a love that had transcended time, mortality, and all boundaries, a love that would endure for eternity.

In the face of the challenges that lay ahead, Elena and Adrian's love remained unyielding, an immortal flame that would continue to burn in a world where love knew no bounds. Their story was a testament to the power of love to conquer all obstacles, to endure through the ages, and to shine as brightly as the stars in the endless expanse of the night.

Chapter 11: The Hunt for Victoria

Elena and Adrian's immortal love had withstood the test of time, but a new threat emerged—one that would challenge their bond and lead them on a perilous journey in pursuit of justice and redemption.

Victoria, a powerful and vengeful vampire, had long harbored a deep-seated hatred for Adrian. Her vendetta stemmed from a centuries-old feud, a blood feud that had left wounds that refused to heal. She blamed Adrian for the loss of her family and her transformation into a vampire against her will.

Determined to exact revenge, Victoria embarked on a relentless campaign to undermine Adrian's influence and reputation within vampire society. She plotted in the shadows, manipulating events to tarnish his name and turn his allies against him.

Elena and Adrian, aware of the danger that Victoria posed, knew that they could not ignore the threat any longer. They were determined to confront their adversary and put an end to the cycle of vengeance that had plagued them for centuries.

Their hunt for Victoria led them on a trail of intrigue and danger, as they delved into the darkest corners of the vampire world. They sought allies among those who had suffered at Victoria's hands and uncovered long-buried secrets that shed light on her true motives.

As they closed in on their elusive prey, the tension grew, and the stakes became higher than ever before. Elena and Adrian's love served as both a source of strength and vulnerability. They knew that Victoria would stop at nothing to tear them apart and that their love made them targets.

One moonlit night, beneath the shadow of an ancient cathedral, Elena and Adrian finally confronted Victoria. The confrontation was a clash of wills and power, a battle that would determine the fate of their eternal love.

Victoria, with her dark powers and unwavering determination, proved to be a formidable adversary. She taunted Elena and Adrian, dredging up painful memories and old wounds. But their love was a force that could not be underestimated, and it fueled their determination to end the cycle of vengeance once and for all.

In a final, epic battle, Elena and Adrian joined forces, their love catalyzing their strength and resilience. Together, they faced Victoria, their powers colliding in a dazzling display of supernatural energy.

As the battle raged on, Elena and Adrian's love shone brighter than ever before. It was a love that defied the darkness and overcame the pain of the past. It was a love that had endured centuries of trials and tribulations, emerging as an unbreakable bond that could withstand any challenge.

In the end, their love proved to be the ultimate weapon against Victoria's hatred and vengeance. They emerged victorious, their adversary defeated, and the cycle of vengeance finally broken.

As they stood together, victorious and united, Elena and Adrian knew that their love had conquered not only the forces of darkness but also the wounds of the past. Their journey had been long and arduous, filled with challenges and sacrifices, but their love had endured, stronger than ever.

The hunt for Victoria had tested the limits of their love and their commitment to justice, but it had also reaffirmed the power of their immortal bond. Their story was a testament to the enduring strength of love in the face of adversity, a love that would shine as brightly as the stars in the endless expanse of the night.

Chapter 12: The Council's Judgment

With Victoria defeated and the cycle of vengeance broken, Elena and Adrian's love story took a new turn—one that would bring them face to face with the highest authority in vampire society, the Council of Elders.

The Council had been watching the events unfold with a keen interest. The rivalry, the hunt for Victoria, and the battle that had ensued had not gone unnoticed. They viewed Elena and Adrian's actions with a mixture of curiosity and concern, their suspicions growing with each passing day.

The Council's judgment held the power to shape the future of Elena and Adrian's love, and they knew that they would have to answer for their actions. The Council convened in a grand hall, a gathering of the most powerful and influential vampires, to pass judgment on the star-crossed lovers.

Elena and Adrian stood before the Council, their hearts heavy with anticipation. The Council's leader, a venerable elder with centuries of wisdom, fixed his piercing gaze upon them. He spoke with a voice that echoed through the chamber, demanding their attention.

"Elena and Adrian," he began, his voice a solemn rumble, "your actions have sent ripples through our society. Your love has defied convention, challenged tradition, and tested the very fabric of our world."

The Council members listened intently, their expressions a mixture of curiosity and judgment.

Elena and Adrian, undaunted, shared their story—their love, their trials, and their determination to be together. They spoke of the sacrifices they had made, the battles they had fought, and the love that had remained unbreakable through the ages.

The Council deliberated, their discussions filled with tension and uncertainty. They weighed the love of Elena and Adrian against the traditions and laws that had governed vampire society for centuries. It was a decision that held the power to change the course of their love story forever.

Finally, the leader of the Council spoke again, his voice carrying the weight of their verdict. "Elena and Adrian, your love has defied the odds and endured through trials that would have broken others. It is a love that has proven itself time and again, a love that transcends time and mortality."

The Council's judgment was clear. They acknowledged the power of Elena and Adrian's love, recognizing it as a force that could not be denied or extinguished. They chose to grant their blessing to the star-crossed lovers, a decision that sent shockwaves through the vampire society.

Elena and Adrian were free to love each other without fear of persecution or reprisal. Their love had triumphed over tradition, and they emerged from the Council's judgment with their heads held high.

As they left the grand hall, hand in hand, they knew that their love story was unlike any other—a story of love that had conquered all obstacles, defied the laws of vampire society, and endured through the ages. Their love was a beacon of hope and defiance, a testament to the power of the heart to overcome even the most formidable challenges.

With the Council's blessing, Elena and Adrian's love story continued to unfold, a tale of immortal love that

would be told for generations to come. It was a love that would shine as brightly as the stars in the endless expanse of the night, a love that would endure for all eternity.

Chapter 13: A New Beginning

With the Council's blessing and the weight of past challenges behind them, Elena and Adrian embarked on a new chapter of their immortal love—a chapter filled with hope, anticipation, and the promise of a future together.

Their love, once marred by rivalry, vendettas, and the specter of vengeance, had emerged triumphant. It had proven itself as a force that defied tradition and transcended time, a love that was unbreakable and eternal.

As they walked through the moonlit streets of Wraithhaven, their hands entwined, Elena and Adrian felt a sense of freedom and possibility that they had never experienced before. They were no longer bound by the constraints of vampire society, and their love was free to flourish without fear of persecution.

Their bond had grown stronger with each trial they had faced, and their love was now a beacon of hope within the vampire world. Other vampires looked to them as an example of what love could be—a love that conquered all obstacles and endured through the ages.

But their journey was far from over, and the future held its own set of challenges and mysteries. They were immortal beings with an eternity ahead of them, and they were determined to make the most of their time together.

Elena and Adrian explored the world, traveling to distant lands and experiencing the beauty of different cultures. They reveled in the joys of human existence, savoring the tastes, sights, and sounds of the mortal world.

They also continued to protect the innocent from the shadows, using their unique abilities to help those in need. Their love had become a source of strength, a force for good in a world filled with darkness.

As the years turned into decades and the decades into centuries, Elena and Adrian's love remained as passionate and unyielding as ever. It was a love that had been tested in the fires of adversity and had emerged stronger for it.

They watched as the world changed around them, witnessed the rise and fall of empires, and saw the evolution of humanity. Through it all, their love remained a constant, an anchor in an ever-shifting world.

Their story became a legend among vampires—a tale of love, resilience, and the enduring power of the heart. It was a story that gave hope to those who believed in the possibility of love that transcended time and mortality.

As they stood together, beneath the eternal gaze of the moon, Elena and Adrian knew that their love was a gift—an immortal gift that would continue to shine brightly in the night, a love that would endure for all eternity.

Their new beginning was a testament to the enduring strength of their love, a love that had overcome the greatest of challenges and would continue to burn as brightly as the stars in the endless expanse of the night.

Chapter 14: A Love Tested

Elena and Adrian's immortal love had endured countless trials and triumphs, but a new challenge arose—one that would push their bond to its limits and test the very essence of their commitment.

Amid their idyllic existence, a series of unexplained disappearances rocked the vampire world. Vampires were vanishing without a trace, leaving behind a trail of fear and uncertainty. The vampire community was in turmoil, and whispers of a sinister force at play spread like wildfire.

Elena and Adrian, ever vigilant and protective of their kind, took it upon themselves to investigate the mysterious disappearances. Their love for each other and their sense of responsibility to their fellow vampires drove them to seek answers.

Their journey led them into the shadowy underbelly of the vampire society, where dark secrets and hidden dangers lurked. They encountered a clandestine organization known as the Nightshade Syndicate—a group of rogue vampires who had discovered a way to imprison and drain the powers of their kin.

The Syndicate's leader, a malevolent vampire known as Sable, saw Elena and Adrian as a threat to his plans. He believed that their love, with its unmatched strength and resilience, posed a danger to his operations. He sought to capture them and use their powers to bolster his own.

Elena and Adrian's investigation soon turned into a deadly game of cat and mouse, as they navigated a web of deception and danger. They faced traps, ambushes, and a constant sense of unease as they delved deeper into the Syndicate's operations.

Their love became a source of strength and resilience in the face of adversity. They leaned on each other for support, their unbreakable bond serving as a beacon of hope in the darkest of times. But the challenges they faced threatened to tear them apart.

In a fateful encounter with Sable and his followers, Elena and Adrian found themselves captured and imprisoned in a hidden fortress. The Syndicate sought to drain their powers and use them for their nefarious purposes, believing that their love would only make them more formidable.

As they languished in captivity, their love was tested as never before. They faced physical and emotional torment, their powers weakening with each passing day. But their determination to protect each other and their fellow vampires remained unwavering.

In a daring escape, Elena and Adrian rallied their strength and fought back against their captors. It was a battle that would determine the fate of not only their love but also the future of the vampire world.

Their powers surged, fueled by their love and determination. The fortress trembled as they unleashed their combined strength, breaking free from their prison and confronting Sable and his followers in a final, epic showdown.

In the end, love triumphed over darkness. Elena and Adrian emerged victorious, defeating the Syndicate and putting an end to the disappearances that had plagued their kind. Their love had been tested in the crucible of adversity, and it had emerged stronger than ever.

As they stood together, surrounded by the ruins of the Syndicate's fortress, Elena and Adrian knew that their love was an unbreakable force—a force that had overcome the darkest of challenges and would continue to shine as brightly as the stars in the endless expanse of the night.

Their story was a testament to the enduring power of love, a love that had conquered all obstacles and endured through the ages. Their immortal bond was a beacon of hope and defiance in a world where love knew no bounds, a love that would endure for all eternity.

Chapter 15: An Ancient Prophecy

In the aftermath of their victory over the Nightshade Syndicate, Elena and Adrian's love story took an unexpected turn—a turn that would lead them to confront an ancient prophecy that had the power to shape the destiny of their immortal love.

The vampire world buzzed with rumors of an age-old prophecy, whispered among vampires for centuries. It spoke of a love that would transcend time and space, a love that would unite vampires and humans in a way never seen before. It was a prophecy that had long been dismissed as legend, but recent events had revived interest in its existence.

Elena and Adrian, ever curious and vigilant, decided to investigate the prophecy themselves. They sought out ancient texts and consulted with vampire sages, determined to uncover the truth behind the enigmatic prophecy.

As they delved deeper into their research, they discovered that the prophecy foretold the emergence of a "Chosen Love"—a love so powerful that it could bridge the divide between vampires and humans, forging a new era of understanding and cooperation.

The prophecy also hinted at the existence of a mystical artifact, known as the "Heartstone," which was said to hold the key to unlocking the Chosen Love's full potential. The Heartstone was believed to be hidden in a remote and treacherous location, and its discovery would be a challenge in itself.

Elena and Adrian, undaunted by the dangers that lay ahead, embarked on a quest to find the Heartstone and fulfill the prophecy. Their love had already defied convention and tradition, and they were eager to explore the possibilities of the Chosen Love.

Their journey took them to distant lands, across forbidding landscapes, and into the heart of uncharted territory. They faced obstacles and trials that tested their resolve, but their love remained a source of strength and determination.

As they neared the location of the Heartstone, they encountered ancient guardians and faced mystical challenges. It became clear that the Heartstone's power was not to be taken lightly, and their love would be tested in ways they could never have anticipated.

In a climactic moment, as they finally uncovered the Heartstone, its radiant energy enveloped them. The artifact recognized the depth of their love and the potential for unity between vampires and humans. It bestowed upon them a new level of power and understanding, cementing their status as the Chosen Love.

Elena and Adrian realized that their love was destined to play a pivotal role in the vampire world, bridging the gap between their kind and humans. They returned to Wraithhaven, their hearts filled with a sense of purpose and destiny.

But the true implications of the prophecy and the power of the Heartstone remained shrouded in mystery. As they stood together, ready to embrace their role as the Chosen Love, they knew that their journey was far from over.

Their love story had taken an unexpected turn, one that would challenge the very foundations of their world and reveal the true potential of their love. They were determined to fulfill the ancient prophecy, for their love was a force that could transcend time and space, a love
that would endure for all eternity.

Chapter 16: The Birth of a Hybrid

As Elena and Adrian embraced their role as the Chosen Love and wielded the power of the Heartstone, their love story took a profound and unexpected turn—one that would lead to the birth of a being that would forever change the course of vampire and human history.

The power of the Heartstone had not only united Elena and Adrian in a bond of unparalleled strength but had also unlocked a new potential within them. They discovered that their love had the unique ability to transcend the boundaries of vampire and human existence.

Elena, still possessing the essence of her humanity, and Adrian, an immortal vampire, found themselves on the brink of a revelation. Their love had the power to create a bridge between their two worlds—a bridge that had never been explored before.

As they delved deeper into the mysteries of the Heartstone, they realized that their love had the potential to give rise to a being that was neither fully vampire nor fully human. It would be a hybrid, a creature born of their love, and it held the promise of a new era of understanding and cooperation between their species.

Elena and Adrian, with their newfound powers and sense of purpose, decided to embrace this unique opportunity. They were ready to bring forth a being that would embody the love that had united them and bridge the divide between vampires and humans.

Their journey led them to ancient rituals and mystic ceremonies that would facilitate the birth of the hybrid. The process was fraught with uncertainty and challenges, and it tested the limits of their love and determination.

In a sacred chamber, beneath the light of a celestial alignment, Elena and Adrian performed the ritual that would give life to the hybrid. Their love served as the catalyst, channeling the energies of the Heartstone and uniting them in a moment of profound connection.

As the ritual reached its zenith, a burst of radiant energy enveloped them, and the hybrid was born. A being of extraordinary beauty and power, it possessed both vampire and human qualities, representing the union of their worlds.

Elena and Adrian cradled their newborn creation, their hearts filled with a sense of awe and wonder. The hybrid's existence was a testament to the enduring power of love to transcend boundaries and bring about change.

Word of the hybrid's birth spread throughout the vampire and human worlds, creating a sense of hope and curiosity. It was a being that had the potential to usher in a new era of understanding and cooperation, a being that held the key to a future where love knew no bounds.

But with the birth of the hybrid came new challenges and responsibilities. Elena and Adrian knew that they would need to guide and protect their creation, ensuring that it would fulfill its destiny as a bridge between their species.

As they looked into the eyes of the hybrid, their hearts filled with love and determination. Their love story had taken an unexpected and extraordinary turn, one that would forever change the course of vampire and human history.

Their journey was far from over, but they faced the future with a sense of purpose and destiny. Their love was a force that could transcend time and space, a love that would endure for all eternity, and now, it had given rise to a being that would carry their legacy into the ages to come.

Chapter 17: A Love Across Centuries

With the birth of the hybrid, Elena and Adrian's love story took on a new dimension—one that spanned centuries and tested the boundaries of time, mortality, and immortality.

Elena and Adrian became the guardians and mentors of the hybrid, guiding it through the complexities of its dual nature. They watched as it grew and matured, its presence serving as a beacon of hope and unity between vampires and humans.

The hybrid's existence began to have a profound impact on the vampire world. It challenged long-held beliefs and traditions, sparking a movement towards greater cooperation and understanding between vampires and humans. Elena and Adrian's love story, once a source of controversy, had become a symbol of unity and hope.

As centuries passed, Elena and Adrian continued to walk the immortal path together, their love enduring through the ages. They witnessed the evolution of the world, the rise and fall of civilizations, and the changing dynamics between vampires and humans.

Their love remained unbreakable, a constant in a world that was in a perpetual state of flux. They faced new challenges and adversaries, but their love served as a source of strength and resilience.

The hybrid, now a leader and advocate for unity, played a pivotal role in shaping the future of vampire and human relations. It worked tirelessly to bridge the gap between the two species, forging alliances and promoting understanding.

Elena and Adrian's love story became a legend—one that transcended time and mortality. It was a story of love that had endured through the ages, a love that had brought about change and transformation in a world where love knew no bounds.

Their love was a testament to the power of the heart to overcome all obstacles, bridge divides, and create a future where love, acceptance, and cooperation reigned.

As they stood together, gazing into the horizon of a new era, Elena and Adrian knew that their love story was one for the ages. It was a love that had spanned centuries, a love that had conquered all challenges, and a love that would endure for all eternity.

Their journey was far from over, but they faced the future with hope and optimism. Their love had transcended time and space, and it would continue to shine as brightly as the stars in the endless expanse of the night.

Chapter 18: The Betrayal

Amid an era marked by unity and understanding between vampires and humans, Elena and Adrian faced an unexpected and devastating betrayal—one that threatened to shatter the foundations of their love.

The vampire-human alliance that had been fostered by the presence of the hybrid had flourished for centuries. Cooperation and coexistence had become the norm, and the world had experienced an unprecedented era of peace.

But hidden in the shadows, a faction of vampires known as the "Crimson Veil" had secretly plotted against the alliance. Led by a charismatic but treacherous vampire named Valeria, they believed that vampires should rule over humans with absolute power and dominance.

Valeria's hatred for the hybrid and its message of unity ran deep. She saw it as a threat to the traditional vampire hierarchy and was determined to extinguish it, along with anyone who supported its ideals.

Elena and Adrian, who had been vocal advocates for the alliance, were seen as obstacles to Valeria's plan. Unbeknownst to them, Valeria had cultivated a network of loyal followers within both the vampire and human communities.

The betrayal came suddenly and violently. On a night when the world should have been celebrating unity, the Crimson Veil launched a coordinated attack. Their forces stormed vampire and human enclaves alike, spreading chaos and destruction.

Elena and Adrian, along with the hybrid, found themselves targeted by Valeria's assassins. It was a battle that they had never anticipated, a battle that pitted their love and ideals against an enemy determined to plunge the world into darkness.

During the chaos, Elena and Adrian's love was put to the ultimate test. They fought side by side, their powers and determination fueling their resistance against the betrayal. The hybrid, too, displayed remarkable courage and strength, defending the ideals of unity and cooperation.

As the battle raged on, Elena and Adrian uncovered the extent of Valeria's treachery. She had manipulated their closest allies, turned friends into enemies, and sown the seeds of discord and mistrust.

The betrayal had struck at the heart of their love, shaking their faith in the world they had worked so hard to build. But it also served as a reminder of the enduring power of their bond.

In a climactic showdown, Elena and Adrian confronted Valeria, their love and determination shining as brightly as ever. The battle between light and darkness reached its zenith, and the fate of the world hung in the balance.

In the end, love prevailed over betrayal. Elena and Adrian, with the support of the hybrid and those who still believed in the ideals of unity, defeated Valeria and the Crimson Veil.

But the scars of the betrayal ran deep. The world had been forever changed, and the trust that had once defined their era of cooperation had been shattered.

Elena and Adrian, along with the hybrid, faced the daunting task of rebuilding what had been broken. Their love remained unyielding, a beacon of hope in a world scarred by betrayal and mistrust.

Their journey was a testament to the enduring power of love to overcome even the darkest of challenges. As they looked to the future, they knew that their love would continue to shine as brightly as the stars in the endless expanse of the night, a love that would endure for all eternity.

Chapter 19: The Final Confrontation

In the aftermath of the betrayal by the Crimson Veil, Elena, and Adrian, along with the hybrid, were faced with the daunting task of rebuilding the world they had fought so hard to protect. The scars of betrayal ran deep, and the trust between vampires and humans had been fractured.

As they worked tirelessly to mend the bonds of unity and cooperation, they knew that a final confrontation with the remnants of the Crimson Veil was inevitable. Valeria and her loyal followers had not been completely defeated, and they continued to scheme in the shadows.

Elena, Adrian, and the hybrid became the focal points of Valeria's

wrath. She was determined to see them eliminated, viewing them as the last vestiges of a threat to her vision of vampire dominance.

The final confrontation came to a head on a moonlit night, in a desolate and ancient battleground. The forces of the Crimson Veil, bolstered by Valeria's relentless determination, clashed with Elena, Adrian, the hybrid, and their allies.

It was a battle of epic proportions, a battle that would determine the fate of the world and the ideals of unity and cooperation. Love and loyalty were pitted against hatred and treachery.

Elena and Adrian's love, as well as the hybrid's unwavering commitment to unity, fueled their determination to prevail. They fought with a fierceness born of love, a love that had endured through the ages and had conquered even the darkest of challenges.

The hybrid, now a symbol of hope and resilience, displayed powers and abilities that surpassed anything the world had ever seen. It was a being born of love and unity, and its strength was a reflection of the ideals it represented.

As the battle reached its climax, Elena and Adrian faced Valeria in a showdown. Their love shone brightly, a beacon of hope in the face of hatred and darkness. The clash of powers and wills was a testament to the enduring strength of their bond.

In a moment of profound sacrifice, Elena and Adrian combined their powers, channeling the energy of the Heartstone and the love that had united them. Their sacrifice created a wave of energy that enveloped Valeria, stripping her of her dark powers and rendering her powerless.

The battle ended, and the forces of the Crimson Veil were defeated. Valeria, once a formidable adversary, was left powerless and defeated. The world had been saved from her vision of domination and chaos.

But victory had come at a great cost. Elena and Adrian, weakened by their sacrifice, knew that they could no longer exist in their current form. Their love, however, remained as strong as ever.

In a bittersweet farewell, Elena and Adrian made the ultimate sacrifice for the greater good. They merged their essences with the Heartstone, becoming ethereal beings of pure love and energy, destined to watch over the world they had fought so hard to protect.

The hybrid, now a symbol of unity and hope, took on the mantle of leadership, guiding vampires and humans toward a future of cooperation and understanding. It was a future born of love, sacrifice, and the enduring power of the heart.

As the world healed and the scars of betrayal began to fade, the legacy of Elena and Adrian's love endured. Their story became a legend—a legend of love that had conquered all obstacles, a love that had transcended time and space, a love that would endure for all eternity.

And so, in the aftermath of the final confrontation, the world stood united, bound together by the ideals of love, unity, and cooperation. The legacy of Elena and Adrian's love lived on, a testament to the enduring power of the heart to overcome even the greatest of challenges, bridge divides, and create a future where love knew no bounds.

Chapter 20: A New Dawn

With the defeat of the Crimson Veil and the legacy of Elena and Adrian's love firmly rooted in the world, a new era of peace, unity, and cooperation dawned. The scars of betrayal had healed, and the world had learned the invaluable lessons of love and resilience.

The hybrid, now a symbol of hope and unity, led the way in forging a brighter future. Vampires and humans worked together, building a world where differences were celebrated, and cooperation was paramount.

The ideals of love, sacrifice, and the enduring power of the heart became the guiding principles of this new world. The legacy of Elena and Adrian's love was celebrated and remembered, reminding all that love could conquer even the darkest of challenges.

The hybrid, born of their love, continued to play a pivotal role in maintaining the fragile peace between the two species. It was a living testament to the possibilities that love and unity could achieve.

Elena and Adrian, as ethereal beings of pure love and energy, watched over the world from the realm of the Heartstone. Their presence was felt in the gentle caress of the wind, the warmth of the sun, and the brilliance of the stars.

Their love story, one that had spanned centuries and transcended the boundaries of time and mortality, had left an indelible mark on the world. It was a story of love that had endured through the ages, a love that had conquered all obstacles, and a love that would endure for all eternity.

As the new dawn bathed the world in its soft light, the legacy of Elena and Adrian's love served as a reminder that love was the most powerful force in the universe. It was a force that could bridge divides, heal wounds, and create a future where love knew no bounds.

And so, in the embrace of this new era, the world stood united, bound together by the enduring legacy of love. It was a legacy that would shine as brightly as the stars in the endless expanse of the night, a legacy that would endure for all eternity, a legacy that would forever be a testament to the power of the heart.

Chapter 21: A Love Eternal

In the embrace of the new era of peace and unity, the legacy of Elena and Adrian's love continued to flourish—a love that had defied the boundaries of time and space, a love that had conquered all challenges, and a love that would endure for all eternity.

The world had been forever transformed by the lessons of their love. Vampires and humans lived side by side, their differences celebrated, and their cooperation flourishing. The ideals of love, sacrifice, and unity had become the cornerstones of society.

The hybrid, born of their love and guided by their legacy, remained a symbol of hope and resilience. It worked tirelessly to maintain the fragile peace, bridging the gap between vampires and humans, and reminding all of the power of love to overcome adversity.

Elena and Adrian, as ethereal beings of pure love and energy, watched over the world from the realm of the Heartstone. Their presence was a source of comfort and inspiration, a reminder that love was the most powerful force in the universe.

Their love story, celebrated throughout the ages, became a beacon of hope for generations to come. It was a story of love that had transcended time and mortality, a story that had changed the world and shaped the course of history.

As the centuries passed, the world continued to evolve, but the legacy of Elena and Adrian's love remained constant. It was a love that had endured through the ages, a love that had stood the test of time, and a love that would forever be a testament to the enduring power of the heart.

And so, in the endless expanse of time, the world stood united and at peace, bound together by the legacy of love. It was a love that would shine as brightly as the stars in the night sky, a love that would endure for all eternity, a love that would forever be a reminder that love knew no bounds—a truly eternal love.

Chapter 22: The Legacy of Love

As the centuries unfolded, the legacy of Elena and Adrian's love continued to shape the world in profound and enduring ways. Their story had become more than just a legend; it had become a living testament to the power of love and unity.

The ideals of love, sacrifice, and cooperation remained at the heart of society. Vampires and humans coexisted harmoniously, their differences celebrated as strengths, and their shared values of love and acceptance bound them together.

The hybrid, now a revered figure, continued to bridge the gap between the two species. Its wisdom and compassion were a guiding light in a world that had learned to cherish the lessons of love.

Elena and Adrian, as ethereal beings of pure love and energy, watched over the world from the realm of the Heartstone. Their presence was a constant reminder of the enduring power of their love—a love that had transcended time, a love that had conquered all obstacles, and a love that had forever changed the course of history.

Their love story had become a cornerstone of culture and art, inspiring countless works of literature, music, and art. It was a story that resonated with people from all walks of life, a story that touched hearts and reminded them of the boundless possibilities of love.

Generations came and went, but the legacy of love remained. It was a legacy that had transformed the world, a legacy that had shaped the destiny of vampire and human relations, and a legacy that had left an indelible mark on the collective consciousness of humanity.

And so, as the world continued to evolve, the legacy of Elena and Adrian's love endured—a love that would shine as brightly as the stars in the night sky, a love that would endure for all eternity, and a love that would forever be a testament to the enduring power of the heart.

In the hearts of people and the annals of history, their love story would forever be cherished as a reminder that love was the greatest force in the universe—a force that could overcome all challenges, bridge all divides, and create a future where love knew no bounds. It was a legacy of love that would never fade, a legacy that would live on for all time.

Chapter 23: A Glimpse into the Future

In the ever-evolving world shaped by the enduring legacy of Elena and Adrian's love, a new chapter unfolded—one that offered a glimpse into the limitless possibilities of the future.

The ideals of love, unity, and cooperation continued to thrive, serving as the foundation of a society where vampires and humans lived in harmony. It was a world where differences were celebrated, and diversity was embraced, a world where the lessons of love had been etched into the very fabric of society.

The hybrid, now a symbol of hope and wisdom, remained a guiding presence. It had become a mentor to new generations, imparting the wisdom of its creators and reminding all of the power of love to bring about positive change.

Elena and Adrian, as ethereal beings of pure love and energy, continued to watch over the world from the realm of the Heartstone. Their presence was a source of comfort and inspiration, a reminder that love was a timeless force that transcended the boundaries of time and space.

The legacy of their love had left an indelible mark on the world, influencing everything from politics and art to science and philosophy. It had become a driving force for progress and understanding, a force that had reshaped the destiny of humanity.

As the years turned into centuries, humanity continued to advance, exploring the depths of space and the mysteries of the cosmos. The legacy of love served as a beacon of hope in the face of the unknown, a reminder that the power of the heart could guide them through even the most challenging of frontiers.

In this glimpse into the future, the world stood on the precipice of discoveries, new adventures, and new horizons. It was a world where love knew no bounds, where the lessons of Elena and Adrian's love continued to inspire generations to come.

And so, as the world stretched out towards the infinite possibilities of the universe, the legacy of their love remained—a love that shone as brightly as the stars in the night sky, a love that endured for all eternity, and a love that would forever be a testament to the enduring power of the heart.

As humanity looked to the future, they did so with the knowledge that love was their greatest ally—a force that could bridge divides, overcome challenges, and create a future where love knew no bounds. It was a glimpse into a future where love reigned supreme, a future filled with endless possibilities, and a future where the legacy of love lived on.

Chapter 24: Forever and Always

In the ever-expanding tapestry of time and love, the story of Elena and Adrian continued to echo through the ages, a testament to the enduring power of their love and the lessons it had imparted to the world.

As the world evolved, so did the legacy of their love. The ideals of unity, acceptance, and cooperation remained at the forefront of society. Vampires and humans lived as equals, their shared values fostering a world of peace and understanding.

The hybrid, now a revered figure in its own right, continued to guide future generations toward the path of harmony. Its wisdom and compassion were a source of inspiration for those who sought to embrace the ideals of love and unity.

Elena and Adrian, as ethereal beings of pure love and energy, continued to watch over the world from the realm of the Heartstone. Their presence was a constant reminder that love transcended time and space, a reminder that love was the most powerful force in the universe.

Their love story had become a symbol of hope and resilience, celebrated in art, literature, and music across the centuries. It was a story that touched the hearts of countless generations, a story that served as a reminder of the boundless potential of love.

As the world continued to advance, humanity embarked on journeys beyond the stars, exploring distant galaxies and unlocking the mysteries of the universe. The legacy of love remained a guiding light in the face of the cosmos, a reminder that love could bridge the vast expanse of space and time.

In this future, where the possibilities were limitless, humanity thrived, fueled by the enduring lessons of love. They looked towards the horizon, where new adventures, discoveries, and challenges awaited, confident in the knowledge that love was their greatest ally.

And so, in the grand tapestry of existence, the story of Elena and Adrian's love continued to weave itself into the very fabric of the universe. It was a love that shone eternally, a love that endured through the ages, and a love that would forever be a testament to the boundless, timeless, and unbreakable power of the heart.

As the universe stretched out before them, humanity journeyed into the infinite with the unwavering belief that love would forever be their guiding star. It was a love that would remain with them, forever and always, a love that transcended the boundaries of time and space, a truly eternal love.

Chapter 25: An Everlasting Romance

In the grand tapestry of existence, the story of Elena and Adrian's love continued to unfold, transcending the boundaries of time and space, and becoming an everlasting romance that defined the very essence of the universe.

As the eons passed, the legacy of their love remained an indomitable force in the world. The ideals of unity, compassion, and cooperation continued to flourish, shaping a world where vampires and humans thrived together, their shared values guiding their journey.

The hybrid, now an icon of wisdom and hope, remained a steadfast advocate for love and unity. Its influence extended beyond generations, nurturing a world where the lessons of Elena and Adrian's love were etched into the hearts of all.

Elena and Adrian, as ethereal beings of pure love and energy, continued to watch over the world from the realm of the Heartstone. Their presence was a timeless reminder that love was the truest, most enduring force in the universe—a force that transcended the constraints of time.

Their love story had become a source of inspiration for artists, writers, and dreamers across the galaxies. It was a story that spoke to the human soul, a story that embodied the limitless potential of love.

As humanity ventured further into the cosmos, exploring distant realms and encountering new civilizations, the legacy of love served as a beacon of hope in the face of the unknown. It was a reminder that love had the power to unite even the most disparate of worlds.

In this never-ending journey of discovery, where mysteries and wonders await at every turn, humanity faced the universe with open hearts, confident in the knowledge that love was their truest companion.

And so, in the timeless expanse of the universe, the story of Elena and Adrian's love continued to unfurl—a love that shone brighter than the stars, a love that defied the passage of time, and a love that would forever be an everlasting romance, a love that endured through all eternity.

As they gazed into the boundless cosmos, humanity knew that love would forever be their guiding light—a love that was, is, and always would be, an everlasting romance that transcended the limits of existence, a love that would forever illuminate their path through the infinite expanse of the universe.

Epilogue: Eternal Embrace

In the infinite expanse of the cosmos, where time and space were but threads in the tapestry of existence, the story of Elena and Adrian's love had become a legend, a timeless saga that continued to inspire and resonate through the ages.

The ideals of love, unity, and cooperation had evolved into a way of life. Vampires and humans coexisted harmoniously, their shared values forging an era of unprecedented peace and prosperity.

The hybrid, now a revered sage of wisdom, watched over future generations, imparting the ageless lessons of love and unity. It was a beacon of hope, a reminder that love could transcend all boundaries and bring forth a world of boundless possibilities.

Elena and Adrian, as ethereal beings of pure love and energy, remained guardians of the Heartstone, their presence a constant reminder that love was a force that knew no limits—a force that transcended the very fabric of reality.

Their love story had become a celestial symphony, a source of inspiration for poets, philosophers, and explorers who sought to understand the mysteries of the universe. It was a story that transcended time, a story that touched the hearts of beings across the galaxies.

As civilizations rose and fell, and as new realms of existence were explored, the legacy of love endured, a guiding light in the ever-expanding cosmos. It was a legacy that had shaped the destiny of countless worlds, a legacy that had brought about an age of enlightenment and understanding.

In this cosmic odyssey, where stars were born and galaxies collided, humanity embraced the boundless possibilities of the universe with open arms, confident in the knowledge that love was their truest companion—a force that could bridge the gaps between galaxies, unite disparate species, and bring forth a future where love reigned supreme.

And so, in the eternal embrace of the cosmos, the story of Elena and Adrian's love continued to unfold—a love that shone as brightly as the universe itself, a love that defied the boundaries of existence, and a love that would forever be an eternal embrace, a love that transcended time and space, a love that would endure for all eternity.

As they ventured into the endless expanse of the cosmos, humanity knew that love would forever be their guiding star—a love that was, is, and always would be, an eternal embrace that bound them together, a love that illuminated their path through the boundless wonders of the universe.

Chapter 1: Cursed Hearts: A Romance in the Haunted Mansion: The Mansion on Willow Street

The night was dark, the air heavy with a sense of foreboding as Anna Sullivan stood at the wrought iron gates of Willow Mansion. Towering trees lined the cobblestone path that led to the imposing structure. Ivy clung to the mansion's stone walls, and the full moon cast eerie shadows on the ornate windows.

As a historian with a penchant for uncovering forgotten secrets, Anna had always been drawn to tales of mystery and intrigue. Willow Mansion, with its reputation for being cursed and haunted, was a story that had piqued her interest for years.

The mansion had stood on Willow Street for centuries, its history shrouded in darkness. Rumors of tragic love stories, unexplained disappearances, and ghostly apparitions had haunted the town for generations. It was a place whispered about in hushed tones, a place that both intrigued and terrified the townsfolk.

Anna had spent countless hours researching the mansion's history, poring over old documents and faded photographs. But it was only recently that she had received an unexpected invitation, an invitation that would bring her face to face with the enigma that was Willow Mansion.

Tonight, as she gazed up at the towering structure, Anna couldn't help but feel a mixture of excitement and trepidation. The moonlight seemed to beckon her forward, urging her to step through the gates and into the unknown.

With a deep breath, she pushed open the creaking gates and walked up the cobblestone path, her footsteps echoing in the stillness of the night. The mansion loomed before her, its dark windows like empty eyes watching her every move.

As Anna reached the massive wooden doors, she hesitated for a moment. The invitation had been cryptic, offering no explanation for why she had been chosen to visit the mansion. But her curiosity and the allure of the unknown were irresistible.

With a trembling hand, she pushed the door open, and it groaned loudly in protest. Anna stepped into the dimly lit foyer, her heart pounding in her chest. The air was thick with dust and the musty scent of old books.

It was then that she heard a voice, soft and haunting, echoing through the mansion's corridors. "Welcome to Willow Mansion, Anna Sullivan," it whispered, sending a chill down her spine.

Anna knew that her journey into the heart of darkness had only just begun, and she couldn't help but wonder what secrets and mysteries awaited her within the haunted walls of the mansion on Willow Street.

Chapter 2: The Mysterious Invitation

Anna's footsteps echoed in the dimly lit foyer as she ventured further into Willow Mansion. The voice that had welcomed her lingered in the air, its haunting quality sending shivers down her spine. She couldn't help but wonder who had spoken those words and why she had been invited to this enigmatic place.

The flickering candlelight cast eerie shadows on the ornate wallpaper, making the mansion's grandeur seem more like a haunting spectacle. Anna's eyes were drawn to a majestic staircase that spiraled upward, disappearing into darkness.

Just as she was about to ascend the staircase, a gust of wind extinguished the candles, plunging the foyer into darkness. Panic welled up within her, but before fear could take hold, a soft glow emanated from the top of the staircase, casting an ethereal light that beckoned her to ascend.

Anna climbed the stairs cautiously, each step echoing through the mansion like a whispered secret. At the top of the staircase, she found herself in a corridor lined with portraits of stern-faced individuals, each seemingly frozen in time.

The corridor led to a grand chamber, the doors of which stood slightly ajar. Anna pushed them open, revealing a room bathed in an eerie, bluish light. At the center of the room, an antique desk held a single envelope with her name elegantly written across it.

Approaching the desk, Anna picked up the envelope and carefully broke the wax seal. Inside, she found a letter written in elegant script:

Dearest Anna,

You have been chosen because of your unwavering curiosity and your relentless pursuit of the truth. Willow Mansion holds secrets that have been hidden for centuries, secrets that are intertwined with your destiny. I implore you to explore this mansion, to uncover its mysteries, and to reveal the love story that has been concealed in its dark corners. You are the key to unraveling the curse that has plagued the Willow family for generations.

Trust in the journey that lies ahead, for it will lead you to a love that transcends time and death.

Yours in the shadows,

An Enigmatic Friend

The words sent a shiver down Anna's spine. Who was this enigmatic friend, and how did they know so much about her? The letter left her with more questions than answers, but one thing was clear—it was an invitation to uncover the truth hidden within Willow Mansion.

With determination in her heart and the letter clutched in her hand, Anna knew that she couldn't turn back now. She would delve deeper into the mansion's mysteries, hoping to uncover the love story that had been concealed for centuries and to understand her role in breaking the curse that had plagued the Willow family.

As Anna continued her exploration of the mansion, she couldn't help but feel that her life had taken an unexpected and thrilling turn—one that would lead her down a path of romance, intrigue, and the unknown.

Chapter 3: A Haunting Presence

As Anna delved further into Willow Mansion, she couldn't shake the feeling of being watched. The mansion's dimly lit corridors seemed to come alive with whispered secrets, and the walls seemed to hold memories of the past that yearned to be uncovered.

She wandered into a room that appeared to be a library, its shelves filled with ancient books and dusty tomes. The air was heavy with the scent of aged paper and leather bindings. As Anna ran her fingers over the spines of the books, she felt a sudden chill and the unmistakable presence of someone—or something—else in the room.

Turning slowly, she saw a faint, ghostly figure standing at the far end of the library. It was a woman, dressed in a gown from a bygone era, her eyes filled with a haunting sadness. The woman's translucent form seemed to shimmer in the dim light.

Anna's heart raced as she gazed at the ghostly apparition. It was the same woman she had seen in the portraits lining the mansion's corridors. The woman's spectral presence seemed to beckon Anna closer, her eyes pleading for understanding.

"Who are you?" Anna whispered, her voice trembling.

The ghostly woman didn't speak, but her presence seemed to convey a sense of longing and sorrow. She gestured toward a dusty old journal that lay on a nearby table, its pages yellowed with age.

Anna approached the journal cautiously and opened it. The pages were filled with elegant handwriting, detailing a tragic love story that had unfolded within the walls of Willow Mansion centuries ago.

As Anna read the words on the pages, she was transported back in time. She saw the forbidden love between a young woman named Isabella Willow and a dashing servant named Samuel. Their love was passionate and fierce, but it was met with fierce opposition from the Willow family.

The journal chronicled their secret meetings, stolen kisses, and the pain of being torn apart. It spoke of a curse that had befallen the Willow family, a curse that had claimed the lives of those who dared to defy tradition and love against all odds.

Tears welled up in Anna's eyes as she read the final entry in the journal, which spoke of a desperate plea for someone to break the curse and set the lovers' spirits free.

Anna realized that she was not alone in her quest to uncover the mansion's mysteries. The ghostly woman, the spirit of Isabella Willow, was reaching out to her for help.

With the journal in hand and a newfound determination, Anna knew that she had a mission—to uncover the truth of the past, to break the curse that had haunted the Willow family, and to bring peace to the restless souls that lingered within Willow Mansion.

As she looked once more at the spectral figure of Isabella, Anna made a silent promise to do everything in her power to fulfill her role in this haunting love story—a love story that transcended time and death, a love story that had drawn her into the heart of Willow Mansion's mysteries.

Chapter 4: The Curse of the Willows

The revelation of the tragic love story between Isabella Willow and Samuel weighed heavily on Anna's heart. As she continued her exploration of Willow Mansion, she couldn't help but wonder about the curse that had plagued the Willow family for generations. What had caused it, and how had it endured for so long?

Anna's search for answers led her to the mansion's extensive archives, a dimly lit room filled with dusty old documents and faded photographs. The pages of family records, letters, and diaries whispered tales of sorrow and despair.

In those archives, Anna unearthed the dark history of the Willow family. Generations ago, the Willows had been a prosperous and respected family, known for their grandeur and wealth. But with prosperity came a heavy burden—the curse.

The curse had been cast upon the Willows by a vengeful witch who had cursed the family for their betrayal. The witch's words were etched into an ancient parchment:

For every forbidden love that blooms within these walls, a curse shall befall the Willows. The love shall wither, the family shall suffer, and the spirits shall be bound in torment.

The curse had manifested in various forms over the centuries—tragic accidents, unexplained deaths, and the torment of restless spirits. It seemed that every time a member of the
Willow family dared to love against tradition, the curse had struck with merciless precision.

Anna couldn't help but feel a deep sense of sympathy for the family's tragic fate. The curse had been a relentless specter, destroying happiness and tearing lovers apart. It was a curse that had endured for far too long, and Anna now understood her role in breaking its malevolent grip.

With determination, Anna resolved to delve deeper into the history of the curse, seeking any clues or rituals that could help her break the spell. She would not rest until she had unraveled the secrets of the curse and found a way to free the spirits that haunted Willow Mansion.

As she left the archives, Anna knew that the path ahead was fraught with danger, but she was undeterred. She was determined to confront the curse head-on and uncover the love story that had been hidden in the mansion's shadows for centuries.

Anna's journey had become a mission to rewrite the destiny of the Willows, to break the chains of the curse, and to bring closure to the restless souls that wandered the haunted halls of Willow Mansion. With the journal of Isabella Willow in her possession and a newfound resolve, she was ready to face the challenges that lay ahead and confront the malevolent forces that sought to keep the curse alive.

Chapter 5: The Ghostly Encounter

As Anna delved deeper into the mysteries of Willow Mansion, the presence of the restless spirits that haunted the mansion became more palpable. She often heard faint whispers and caught glimpses of shadowy figures out of the corner of her eye.

One night, as she was exploring a dimly lit corridor, Anna felt a cold breeze brush past her, carrying with it a melancholic whisper. She followed the eerie sound to a doorway that led to a grand ballroom.

The ballroom was bathed in the soft glow of moonlight streaming in through the ornate windows. Anna's breath caught as she saw the figure of a woman in a flowing gown, her silhouette dancing gracefully across the room. It was the same ghostly woman she had encountered earlier—the spirit of Isabella Willow.

Isabella's spectral form moved with ethereal grace, her movements echoing the wistful melody of a long-forgotten waltz. Anna watched in awe as the ghostly dance unfolded before her, a dance that seemed to transcend time itself.

As the haunting waltz continued, Anna noticed another figure joining the spectral dance—a man in period attire, his eyes locked in a loving gaze with Isabella. It was Samuel, Isabella's forbidden love.

The ghostly couple moved as one, their movements filled with longing and desire. Anna couldn't tear her eyes away from the bittersweet spectacle. It was as if the spirits of Isabella and Samuel were reliving the moments of their love, a love that had been torn asunder by the curse.

The room seemed to come alive with the emotions of the past—passion, sorrow, and the unbreakable bond between the two lovers. It was a love that had defied societal norms and had paid a heavy price.

Anna's heart ached as she watched the spectral dance, her own emotions becoming entwined with those of the ghostly couple. She felt a deep empathy for their plight, for the curse that had kept them trapped within the mansion's walls for centuries.

As the waltz came to an end, Isabella and Samuel faded into the moonlight, leaving Anna standing alone in the ballroom. The echoes of their love lingered in the air, a haunting reminder of the tragedy that had befallen them.

Anna knew that she was not merely an observer in this ghostly romance; she was a participant, bound by destiny to help free the spirits of Isabella and Samuel from their eternal torment. The encounter with the ghostly lovers deepened her resolve to confront the curse head-on, uncover the truth of their love, and find a way to break the malevolent spell that held them captive.

With the knowledge of the past and the presence of the spirits guiding her, Anna continued her quest to unravel the mysteries of Willow Mansion, determined to bring closure to the love story that had been trapped in the shadows for far too long.

Chapter 6: Secrets of the Mansion

Anna's determination to uncover the secrets of Willow Mansion grew with each passing day. The spectral encounters and the ghostly presence of Isabella and Samuel had drawn her deeper into the enigma that surrounded the cursed mansion.

She spent hours poring over old documents, journals, and diaries in the mansion's archives, searching for clues that might help her break the curse. It was during one of these late-night research sessions that she stumbled upon a hidden compartment within an ancient oak desk.

Inside the compartment, she discovered a collection of letters—letters that had been carefully preserved over the centuries. The letters were written in delicate script, and their faded pages bore the scent of roses.

As Anna read the letters, she realized that they were love letters exchanged between Isabella and Samuel. The letters spoke of stolen moments, secret rendezvous, and a love that had defied the boundaries of society and class. It was a love that had burned passionately despite the curse that threatened to tear them apart.

In one particularly poignant letter, Isabella had written:

"My dearest Samuel,

With each passing day, my love for you deepens, and I am willing to risk everything to be with you. Our love is a flame that cannot be extinguished, even by the darkest of curses. I pray that one day, we will find a way to break free from this torment and be together, for eternity.

Yours forever,

Isabella"

The letters spoke of a love that had endured through the ages, a love that had transcended time and death. Anna realized that this love story held the key to breaking the curse and setting the spirits of Isabella and Samuel free.

With the letters in hand, Anna continued her exploration of the mansion, searching for any hidden chambers or secret passages that might hold further clues. She knew that the answers lay within the mansion's walls, waiting to be uncovered.

As she delved deeper into her research, Anna began to uncover other secrets of the mansion—hidden compartments, concealed doorways, and forgotten chambers. It seemed that Willow Mansion held more mysteries than she could have ever imagined.

With each secret she uncovered, Anna felt a step closer to unraveling the curse that had plagued the Willow family for generations. She was determined to piece together the puzzle of the mansion's history, to understand the origins of the curse, and to find a way to break its malevolent grip.

The secrets of Willow Mansion were slowly being revealed, and Anna knew that her journey was far from over. As she continued her exploration, she couldn't help but wonder what other hidden truths lay in wait, and how they would ultimately lead her to the redemption and freedom of the spirits that lingered in the haunted halls of the mansion.

Chapter 7: Echoes of the Past

With the love letters between Isabella and Samuel in her possession, Anna felt a renewed sense of purpose in her quest to break the curse of Willow Mansion. The letters were a testament to the enduring love that had defied time, and they held the key to understanding the depths of the curse.

As Anna continued her exploration of the mansion, she couldn't shake the feeling that the spirits of Isabella and Samuel were guiding her. Their presence was no longer limited to fleeting glimpses and spectral encounters; it was as if they were walking beside her, whispering secrets of the past.

One evening, as she wandered through the mansion's grand ballroom, Anna heard a faint echo of laughter—a sound that seemed to resonate with joy and mirth. It was a stark contrast to the melancholic presence that had haunted her until now.

Following the echoes of laughter, Anna was led to a dusty old mirror that adorned one of the ballroom's walls. The mirror, though aged and tarnished, seemed to hold a peculiar allure. Anna approached it cautiously, her reflection blending with the faded images of those who had stood before it in centuries past.

As she gazed into the mirror, the world around her seemed to shift and blur, and for a brief moment, she saw the ballroom come alive with splendor and opulence. It was as though she had been transported back in time, to an era when the mansion had been filled with guests in elegant attire, dancing and reveling in the grandeur of the Willow family.

Among the dancers, Anna recognized the figures of Isabella and Samuel, their eyes locked in a passionate embrace. The echo of their laughter filled the room as they twirled in each other's arms, defying the curse that threatened to tear them apart.

The mirror had become a window to the past, allowing Anna to witness the love story of Isabella and Samuel as it had once unfolded. She watched in awe as their love transcended the boundaries of time, their spirits forever entwined in an eternal dance.

But the vision in the mirror also revealed a darker truth. Anna saw the moment when the curse had descended upon the lovers, shrouding them in darkness and despair. It was a curse that had taken its toll on generations of the Willow family, and it had been cast by a vengeful witch who had sought retribution for a betrayal.

As the vision in the mirror faded, Anna was left with a deeper understanding of the curse's origins and the pain it had caused. She knew that breaking the curse would not be easy, but she was more determined than ever to unravel its malevolent grip.

With the love letters, the echoes of the past, and the mirror's revelations, Anna was armed with knowledge and resolve. She was ready to confront the curse head-on, to rewrite the destiny of the Willows, and to bring an end to the torment
that had plagued the mansion for far too long.

As she left the ballroom, Anna couldn't help but feel that the spirits of Isabella and Samuel were guiding her towards a greater truth, one that held the key to their salvation and the redemption of the mansion itself.

Chapter 8: The Enigmatic Portrait

Anna's exploration of Willow Mansion had led her to uncover many of its secrets, but there was one room she had yet to fully explore—the portrait gallery. The gallery was said to house generations of Willow family portraits, each telling a story of the family's history.

As she entered the gallery, Anna was struck by the sheer number of portraits that lined the walls. The faces of the Willows stared back at her, each with a unique expression and story to tell. It was clear that this room held a wealth of information about the mansion's past.

As Anna moved through the gallery, one particular portrait caught her eye. It was a painting of a young woman with striking, dark eyes and a wistful smile. Her resemblance to Isabella Willow was uncanny. Anna felt an immediate connection to the portrait as if the woman in the painting were reaching out to her.

The plaque beneath the portrait identified the subject as "Victoria Willow." Anna's curiosity was piqued. She had heard no mention of Victoria in her research, and yet there she was, captured in a portrait that seemed to hold a story of its own.

Anna decided to delve deeper into Victoria's story. She searched for any documents or records related to her, hoping to uncover the missing piece of the puzzle. It was during her research that she stumbled upon an old diary—Victoria's diary.

The diary revealed a complex and enigmatic character. Victoria had been the younger sister of Isabella Willow, and her life had been overshadowed by the tragic love story of her sister and Samuel. Victoria's diary was filled with entries that spoke of her love for Samuel, a love that had remained unrequited as he had been devoted to her sister, Isabella.

Victoria's diary entries revealed a deep longing and jealousy, and it became clear that her feelings had played a significant role in the curse that had befallen the Willows. Her unrequited love and the bitterness that had consumed her had contributed to the curse's malevolent power.

As Anna read through Victoria's diary, she couldn't help but feel sympathy for the young woman. Her unfulfilled love had driven her to desperate measures, including seeking the help of a vengeful witch to win Samuel's affections.

The diary also hinted at a hidden chamber within the mansion, a chamber that held the key to the curse's origins and the means to break it. Anna knew that she had to find this chamber and uncover the truth of what had transpired within Willow Mansion.

Armed with the knowledge from Victoria's diary, Anna continued her quest, determined to locate the hidden chamber and confront the curse head-on. The enigmatic portrait of Victoria had opened a new chapter in her investigation, and she was determined to uncover the secrets that lay hidden within the mansion's walls, even if it meant confronting the darker aspects of the Willow family's history.

Chapter 9: A Love Unearthed

Anna's quest to uncover the secrets of Willow Mansion had taken an unexpected turn with the discovery of Victoria Willow's diary. As she delved deeper into the mansion's history, she became increasingly aware of the complex web of emotions that had shaped the lives of the Willow family.

With the diary in hand, Anna set out to search for the hidden chamber mentioned in Victoria's writings—the chamber that was said to hold the key to breaking the curse that had tormented the Willows for generations.

Her search led her to a long-forgotten corridor hidden behind a tapestry. The corridor was dimly lit, and the air was heavy with the scent of aged wood and dust. Anna's footsteps echoed as she moved deeper into the unknown, following the cryptic directions outlined in Victoria's diary.

At the end of the corridor, Anna discovered a concealed door, its surface covered in intricate carvings and symbols. It was clear that this door held the entrance to the hidden chamber that had remained sealed for centuries.

With trembling hands, Anna pushed open the door, revealing a chamber bathed in a soft, eerie light. The room was filled with relics of the past—ancient books, dusty manuscripts, and artifacts that hinted at a forgotten era.

In the center of the chamber stood an ornate pedestal, upon which rested a beautifully crafted amulet. The amulet was adorned with intricate engravings and gemstones that shimmered in the unearthly light. It was a relic of immense power and significance.

Anna recognized the amulet from her research. It was said to be the key to breaking the curse, a talisman that could harness the forces of love and redemption. With the amulet in her hand, she felt a surge of hope and determination.

As she examined the amulet, Anna noticed an inscription on its back—a message of love and forgiveness. It was a message from Isabella and Samuel to Victoria, a plea for her to let go of the bitterness and hatred that had fueled the curse.

With newfound purpose, Anna knew that the time had come to confront the curse head-on. She believed that the amulet held the power to break the malevolent spell and bring peace to the spirits of Isabella, Samuel, and Victoria.

As she left the hidden chamber with the amulet in her possession, Anna couldn't help but feel that she was on the brink of a discovery that would change the fate of Willow Mansion forever. The love story that had been buried in the shadows was about to be unearthed, and the curse that had plagued the Willows for centuries was on the verge of being shattered.

With the amulet as her guide and the spirits of the mansion as her allies, Anna was ready to embark on the final leg of her journey—a journey that would test her courage, her resolve, and her belief in the power of love and redemption. The destiny of Willow Mansion was in her hands, and she was determined to rewrite its history and bring an end to the torment that had haunted its halls for far too long.

Chapter 10: Unraveling the Curse

With the amulet in her possession, Anna was prepared to confront the curse that had plagued Willow Mansion for centuries. She knew that the time had come to unravel the malevolent grip that had torn apart the lives of the Willow family and bound the spirits of Isabella, Samuel, and Victoria to the mansion.

Anna's research revealed that the amulet held the power to harness the forces of love and forgiveness—a power that could break the curse and bring peace to the restless souls. She believed that by following the guidance of the spirits and the messages of love and redemption, she could fulfill her destiny and rewrite the mansion's tragic history.

As she entered the grand ballroom, the heart of the mansion, Anna felt a sense of both trepidation and hope. It was in this very room that she had witnessed the spectral dance of Isabella and Samuel, a dance that had transcended time and death. It was a place filled with echoes of the past, a place that held the memories of love and suffering.

With the amulet clutched tightly in her hand, Anna began a ritual guided by the messages she had uncovered in Victoria's diary and the inscription on the amulet. She spoke words of love, forgiveness, and redemption, calling upon the spirits of the mansion to hear her plea.

As she spoke, the room seemed to come alive with an otherworldly energy. The chandeliers flickered, and a soft, haunting melody filled the air. Anna could feel the presence of Isabella, Samuel, and Victoria, their spirits drawn to the ritual that held the promise of freedom.

Suddenly, the room was enveloped in a bluish light, and the figures of Isabella, Samuel, and Victoria materialized before Anna. Their ghostly forms were filled with both longing and hope, their eyes fixed on the amulet in her hand.

Anna continued to speak the words of love and forgiveness, urging the spirits to let go of their pain and bitterness. She reminded them of the love that had once bound them together and the tragedy that had torn them apart. She implored them to find peace and redemption in the power of the amulet.

As the ritual reached its climax, the amulet began to glow with a brilliant light, its gemstones radiating with a warmth that seemed to cleanse the room of darkness. The spirits of Isabella, Samuel, and Victoria were bathed in the light, and Anna could see the anguish in their eyes slowly give way to acceptance and forgiveness.

With a final, powerful surge of energy, the amulet released a burst of light that enveloped the spirits. Anna watched in awe as Isabella, Samuel, and Victoria began to ascend, their forms becoming more ethereal with each passing moment. They seemed to be ascending towards a brighter realm, finally free from the curse that had bound them.

As the light dissipated, Anna was left standing alone in the ballroom, her heart filled with a profound sense of accomplishment and relief. The curse that had haunted Willow Mansion for generations had been broken, and the spirits of the past had found peace and redemption.

The mansion itself seemed to respond to the change. The atmosphere in the room shifted, and the heavy, oppressive feeling that had lingered for centuries was replaced by a sense of serenity and tranquility.

Anna knew that her mission had been fulfilled and that the love story of Isabella, Samuel, and Victoria had finally found its resolution. The destiny of Willow Mansion had been rewritten, and the mansion itself seemed to breathe a sigh of relief.

As Anna left the ballroom, she couldn't help but feel a profound connection to the spirits and the history of the mansion. Her journey had been one of discovery, redemption, and the power of love to transcend even the darkest of curses.

With the curse lifted, Willow Mansion would no longer be a place of tragedy and despair, but a place where the echoes of the past could finally rest in peace. Anna's role in the mansion's history was complete, and she knew that she would carry the love story of Isabella, Samuel, and Victoria with her—a reminder of the enduring power of love and the ability to rewrite even the most tragic of destinies.

Chapter 11: The Midnight Waltz

In the wake of breaking the curse, Willow Mansion underwent a profound transformation. The once-oppressive atmosphere gave way to a newfound serenity, and the mansion seemed to embrace a sense of peace that had long eluded it. Anna's role in rewriting its destiny had left an indelible mark on the grand estate.

As the days turned to weeks, Anna found herself drawn to the grand ballroom once more—the very room where she had witnessed the spectral dance of Isabella and Samuel. It was a place now imbued with a sense of hope and renewal, and Anna couldn't resist the allure of the room that had been at the heart of her journey.

One night, unable to sleep, Anna decided to visit the ballroom. The moonlight streamed in through the windows, casting a soft, ethereal glow upon the polished floor. She stood there, gazing at the spot where Isabella and Samuel had once danced.

As she watched, a gentle breeze seemed to fill the room, and the haunting melody of a waltz echoed through the air. It was as though the spirits of the mansion were inviting her to join in their dance—a dance of celebration and joy.

Anna hesitated for a moment, then took a step forward. The music seemed to envelop her, and she felt as though she were being guided by unseen hands. She began to move gracefully across the floor, her steps synchronized with the haunting waltz.

It was a dance that transcended time and space, a dance that connected her to the spirits of Isabella, Samuel, and Victoria. With each turn and twirl, Anna felt a profound sense of unity with the love story that had unfolded within the mansion's walls.

As the waltz continued, Anna felt a presence beside her. She turned, and there before her stood the spectral forms of Isabella and Samuel. Their eyes were filled with gratitude and happiness, and they joined her in the dance, their ethereal forms moving with a grace that seemed to defy the boundaries of the mortal world.

The three of them danced together in the moonlit ballroom, their spirits intermingling with the music and the history of the mansion. It was a moment of profound connection, a moment that spoke of redemption and the power of love to endure beyond death.

As the waltz came to an end, Anna found herself standing alone once more, her heart filled with a deep sense of fulfillment. She knew that her journey had come full circle and that she had not only broken the curse but had also forged a bond with the spirits of Willow Mansion.

The mansion itself seemed to respond to the midnight waltz as if acknowledging the role Anna had played in rewriting its history. It was a place transformed, a place where the echoes of the past now whispered tales of love and redemption.

As Anna left the ballroom, she knew that she would carry the memory of the midnight waltz with her always—a reminder of the enduring power of love, the ability to rewrite destiny, and the profound connection between the living and the spirits of the past.

Willow Mansion had found its peace, and Anna had found her sense of purpose and belonging in the world. Her journey had been a testament to the extraordinary, a tale of love that had transcended time and death—a tale that would forever linger in the halls of Willow Mansion, waiting to be discovered by those who dared to enter its enigmatic embrace.

Chapter 12: The Ghostly Whispers

With the curse broken and the spirits of Willow Mansion at peace, Anna's life took on a sense of normalcy once more. The mansion once shrouded in darkness, now exuded an air of tranquility and serenity.

But Anna couldn't forget the profound connection she had forged with the spirits of the mansion during her journey. Even as she went about her daily life, she felt their presence as a comforting and guiding force. It was as if Isabella, Samuel, and Victoria watched over her, their love and gratitude echoing in the stillness of the mansion.

One evening, as Anna sat in the mansion's library, she heard faint whispers—a soft, melodic voice that seemed to come from nowhere and yet everywhere. It was a voice she recognized immediately as Isabella's.

"Thank you," Isabella's voice whispered, its ethereal quality sending shivers down Anna's spine. "You have given us the gift of freedom and love."

Tears welled in Anna's eyes as she responded softly, "You're welcome, Isabella. It was an honor to help you find peace."

The whispers continued, and Anna found herself engaged in a conversation with the spirits of the mansion. They shared stories of their lives, their hopes, and their dreams—stories that had been trapped in the shadows for centuries.

As the days passed, Anna became more attuned to the ghostly whispers. She learned about the history of the mansion, the generations of Willows who had called it home, and the profound impact of the curse on their lives. It was a history filled with love, tragedy, and the enduring power of the human spirit.

Anna also discovered that the mansion held more secrets than she had initially realized. The spirits guided her to hidden passages, forgotten chambers, and concealed treasures that had been lost to time. It was as though the mansion itself was eager to share its history with her.

One day, while exploring a dusty attic, Anna uncovered a chest filled with old letters, diaries, and artifacts that shed light on the lives of the Willows. She realized that her connection with the spirits had become a mission—to preserve the history of the mansion and the stories of its inhabitants.

With determination, Anna set out to document the history of Willow Mansion, compiling the stories, letters, and diaries she had uncovered. She knew that it was a task that would take time and effort, but it was a labor of love—one that would ensure that the memories of the mansion and its inhabitants would endure for generations to come.

As she continued to converse with the spirits and uncover the secrets of the mansion, Anna felt a profound sense of gratitude and fulfillment. She had not only broken the curse but had also forged a lasting bond with the spirits of Willow Mansion.

The ghostly whispers were no longer whispers of sorrow and despair; they were whispers of love, gratitude, and the enduring power of the human spirit. And as Anna carried out her mission to preserve the mansion's history, she knew that she was not alone—she was accompanied by the spirits who had found their peace, and by the love story that had transcended time and death.

Willow Mansion had been transformed from a place of darkness into a place of light and redemption, and Anna had played a pivotal role in its remarkable journey.

Chapter 13: The Love Letters

Anna's connection with the spirits of Willow Mansion continued to deepen, and she dedicated herself to preserving the history of the mansion and the stories of the Willow family. As she delved further into her mission, she stumbled upon a collection of love letters—letters that revealed a love story beyond even that of Isabella, Samuel, and Victoria.

The letters were hidden away in a forgotten attic trunk, their delicate pages yellowed with age. They were addressed to a woman named Eleanor, and they bore the signature of a mysterious suitor named Alexander.

As Anna read the first letter, she was transported back in time to an era when quill pens and inkwells were the tools of romantic expression. The words on the page were filled with passion, longing, and a profound sense of love.

"My Dearest Eleanor,

With each passing day, my heart yearns for your presence. The very thought of you fills my hours with warmth and light. The world may be vast and uncertain, but in your eyes, I have found my home. I long for the day when I can hold you in my arms and declare my love for you.

Yours Forever,

Alexander"

As Anna read through the letters, she realized that Eleanor and Alexander's love story had unfolded within the very walls of Willow Mansion. Their love had been a secret, a forbidden romance that had defied societal expectations and familial disapproval.

Eleanor had been a servant in the mansion, while Alexander had been a member of the Willow family. Their love had been a hidden flame, burning with intensity despite the obstacles that stood in their way.

The letters spoke of stolen moments in hidden chambers, clandestine meetings under the moonlit sky, and a love that had endured against all odds. Anna felt a deep connection to their story, as it mirrored the themes of love, secrecy, and redemption that had defined her journey.

As she continued to uncover Eleanor and Alexander's love letters, Anna realized that their love story had also been affected by the curse that had haunted the mansion. The letters hinted at a tragic ending—a separation forced by circumstances beyond their control.

Determined to uncover the truth, Anna embarked on a quest to trace the footsteps of Eleanor and Alexander within the mansion. She followed the clues left behind in the letters, searching for the hidden chambers and secret rendezvous spots where their love had blossomed.

With each discovery, Anna felt a growing connection to the spirits of Eleanor and Alexander. Their love story had been a testament to the enduring power of love, even in the

face of adversity. It was a story that deserved to be told and preserved, just as she had done for Isabella, Samuel, and Victoria.

As Anna delved deeper into the secrets of Eleanor and Alexander's love, she couldn't help but wonder if their story held the key to another layer of the mansion's history, one that had remained hidden for centuries. With determination and a sense of purpose, she set out to uncover the truth and ensure that their love story, like that of Isabella and Samuel, would endure as a testament to the enduring power of love and redemption within the walls of Willow Mansion.

Chapter 14: A Shared Dream

Anna's quest to uncover the hidden love story of Eleanor and Alexander had become a mission close to her heart. The love letters she had discovered in the attic trunk had transported her back in time, and she felt a deep connection to the forbidden romance that had unfolded within the walls of Willow Mansion.

As she followed the clues from the letters, Anna was led to a forgotten chamber deep within the mansion. The room was shrouded in darkness, and cobwebs adorned its corners as if it had been untouched for centuries.

In the center of the chamber stood an old, ornate mirror—a mirror that seemed to hold a mysterious allure. Anna approached it cautiously, her heart racing with anticipation. She had learned from the love letters that this mirror had played a pivotal role in the secret meetings between Eleanor and Alexander.

As she gazed into the mirror, the world around her began to shift and blur, and she felt herself being transported back in time to an era when Eleanor and Alexander's love had blossomed.

Before her eyes, she saw the reflection of a young woman with a radiant smile—Eleanor. Her eyes sparkled with love and anticipation as she stood before the mirror, awaiting a clandestine rendezvous with Alexander.

Moments later, the reflection of a young man appeared beside Eleanor—a dashing figure with a strong resemblance to the Willow family. It was Alexander, and his eyes were filled with a deep, unwavering love as he took Eleanor's hand.

The mirror had become a portal to the past, allowing Anna to witness the moments when Eleanor and Alexander's love had flourished. She watched as they declared their love for each other, exchanged stolen kisses, and shared dreams of a future.

But the vision in the mirror also revealed the challenges they had faced—the disapproval of the Willow family, the societal constraints of their time, and the looming presence of the curse that had haunted the mansion.

Anna could feel the intensity of their love and the desperation of their circumstances. Their love had been a shared dream—a dream that had sustained them through the darkest of times.

As the vision in the mirror faded, Anna knew that she had a responsibility to ensure that Eleanor and Alexander's love story was not forgotten. Their love had endured against all odds, and it deserved to be celebrated and preserved, just like the love story of Isabella, Samuel, and Victoria.

With a renewed sense of purpose, Anna set out to document the love story of Eleanor and Alexander, using the love letters, the hidden chamber, and the mirror as her guide. She was determined to ensure that their shared dream would endure as a testament to the enduring power of love and the ability to transcend the boundaries of time and adversity.

As she left the chamber, Anna couldn't help but feel a profound connection to the spirits of Eleanor and Alexander. Their love story had become her own, and she was committed to sharing it with the world—a story of love, courage, and the unbreakable bond between two souls who had dared to dream in the face of the unknown.

Chapter 15: The Curse's Grip

Anna's mission to document the love story of Eleanor and Alexander had become an all-consuming passion. She was determined to ensure that their shared dream would endure as a testament to the enduring power of love and redemption.

As she delved deeper into her research, Anna uncovered more letters, diaries, and artifacts that shed light on the lives of Eleanor and Alexander. Their love had been a secret, a forbidden romance that had defied societal expectations and familial disapproval.

But as Anna delved further into their story, she began to sense a darkness that had lurked in the background—a darkness that seemed to be intertwined with the curse that had haunted Willow Mansion for generations.

Eleanor and Alexander's love story faced countless obstacles, from the disapproval of the Willow family to the societal constraints of their time. But there was something more, something sinister that had cast a shadow over their love.

The love letters hinted at a malevolent force that had sought to keep Eleanor and Alexander apart. It was a force that seemed to thrive on their love and desperation, feeding on their pain and torment.

Anna couldn't ignore the feeling that the curse that had haunted the mansion for centuries was not limited to the tragedy of Isabella, Samuel, and Victoria. It was a curse that had woven itself into the very fabric of the mansion, ensnaring all who had dared to love within its walls.

Determined to uncover the truth, Anna turned to the spirits of the mansion for guidance. She sought their help in understanding the origins of the curse and its hold on Eleanor and Alexander.

One evening, as she sat in the mansion's library, she heard the whispers of the spirits—a chorus of voices filled with sorrow and regret. They spoke of a vengeful presence that had taken root in the mansion, a presence that sought to destroy love and happiness.

Anna realized that the curse had not only torn apart the lives of Isabella, Samuel, and Victoria but had also extended its malevolent reach to Eleanor and Alexander. It was a curse that fed on the pain and suffering of those who dared to love, trapping their spirits within the mansion's walls.

As Anna continued her quest to unravel the curse's grip, she couldn't help but wonder if breaking the curse of Eleanor and Alexander would be the key to liberating the mansion from its dark legacy once and for all. The shadows of the past seemed to close in around her, and she knew that the battle against the curse was far from over.

With determination and a sense of purpose, Anna set out to confront the curse head-on, armed with the love letters, the hidden chambers, and the spirits of the mansion as her allies. She was determined to rewrite the destiny of Willow Mansion and to free the souls of those who had been trapped by the curse's malevolent grip.

The mansion's history was a tapestry of love and tragedy, and Anna was determined to change its course, to break the curse's hold, and to ensure that love would finally triumph over darkness within the walls of Willow Mansion.

Chapter 16: The Forgotten Journal

As Anna continued her quest to confront the curse's grip on Willow Mansion, she felt a growing sense of urgency. The shadows of the past seemed to close in around her, and she knew that she was on the brink of uncovering the truth that had eluded her for so long.

One day, while exploring the mansion's hidden passages, Anna stumbled upon a dusty old journal. Its leather cover was worn and weathered, and its pages were yellowed with age. It was a journal that had been forgotten, hidden away from prying eyes.

As she opened the journal, Anna realized that it belonged to a member of the Willow family—an ancestor who had lived during the time of Eleanor and Alexander. The journal contained detailed accounts of the events that had transpired within the mansion, as well as the author's observations and suspicions.

The entries in the journal hinted at a dark secret that had been carefully concealed—a secret that was at the heart of the curse that had plagued the mansion for generations. The author wrote of strange occurrences, unexplained phenomena, and a malevolent force that seemed to thrive on the suffering of the inhabitants.

Anna's heart raced as she read through the journal. It was as though the author had been on a quest similar to her own—a quest to understand the origins of the curse and to break its grip on the mansion.

The journal also contained references to a hidden chamber—a chamber that was said to hold the key to the curse's origins. It was a chamber that had eluded Anna's previous searches, but now she had a clear lead.

With determination and a sense of purpose, Anna set out to locate the hidden chamber described in the journal. She followed the clues left behind by the author, searching for secret passages and concealed entrances.

After days of meticulous searching, Anna finally discovered the entrance to the hidden chamber. It was a door hidden behind a bookshelf in the mansion's library, its existence known only to a select few.

As she entered the chamber, Anna felt a chill in the air—a palpable sense of darkness and malevolence that seemed to emanate from the very walls. The chamber was filled with ancient tomes, artifacts, and symbols that hinted at a sinister purpose.

In the center of the chamber stood a pedestal, upon which rested an ornate box. It was a box of exquisite craftsmanship, adorned with intricate engravings and symbols that seemed to pulse with an otherworldly energy.

Anna realized that this box held the key to the curse's origins—a key that could unlock the mysteries of the mansion's dark legacy. With trembling hands, she opened the box, revealing a collection of ancient scrolls and manuscripts.

As she began to decipher the writings, Anna uncovered the truth that had been hidden for centuries. The curse that had haunted Willow Mansion was not a mere coincidence; it was a result of a vengeful pact made by a member of the Willow family—an ancestor who had
sought power and immortality at a terrible cost.

The curse had been fueled by the suffering of those who had dared to love within the mansion's walls, and its malevolent force had grown stronger with each passing generation.

Anna knew that she had uncovered the key to breaking the curse once and for all. With the knowledge contained within the scrolls, she could confront the vengeful presence that had ensnared the mansion and its inhabitants.

Armed with the truth, Anna set out to prepare for a final confrontation with the curse—a battle that would test her courage, her resolve, and her unwavering belief in the power of love and redemption. The destiny of Willow Mansion hung in the balance, and Anna was determined to free the spirits of those who had suffered for far too long.

Chapter 17: The Seance

Armed with the knowledge of the curse's origins, Anna knew that the time had come for a final confrontation with the malevolent force that had haunted Willow Mansion for centuries. She had uncovered the truth hidden within the forgotten journal and the ancient scrolls, and she was determined to break the curse's grip once and for all.

Anna gathered the spirits of the mansion—Isabella, Samuel, Victoria, Eleanor, and Alexander—around her in the grand ballroom. The spirits had become her allies, their ethereal presence a source of strength and guidance.

With the moonlight streaming in through the windows, Anna prepared for a seance—a ritual that would allow her to communicate with the vengeful presence that had ensnared the mansion. She had learned from the journal that the curse was a sentient force, a malevolent entity that fed on the suffering of those who had dared to love within the mansion's walls.

As she lit candles and arranged a circle of protective symbols, Anna felt a sense of trepidation. She knew that she would be facing a powerful and vengeful force, one that would stop at nothing to protect its hold on the mansion.

The spirits of the mansion stood beside her, their presence a source of reassurance. They were united in their desire to see the curse broken and the mansion liberated from its dark legacy.

As the seance began, Anna called out to the malevolent force, invoking its presence and demanding answers. The room seemed to come alive with a palpable energy, and the candles flickered in response.

Suddenly, a cold wind swept through the ballroom, and the atmosphere grew heavy with an oppressive darkness. The malevolent force revealed itself—a swirling, shadowy figure that seemed to defy the laws of nature.

It spoke with a voice that echoed with malice and contempt, taunting Anna and the spirits. It accused them of meddling in affairs beyond their understanding and vowed to continue its reign of torment.

But Anna was undeterred. She had the truth on her side, and she knew that the curse's power was not absolute. With the knowledge contained within the ancient scrolls, she began to recite incantations and rituals designed to weaken the curse's hold.

As the rituals unfolded, the malevolent force began to waver, its shadowy form flickering like a dying flame. It let out a deafening scream of anguish and despair, and Anna could feel the mansion itself responding to the battle that raged within its walls.

With a final surge of determination, Anna and the spirits of the mansion channeled their collective energy into a powerful burst of light that engulfed the malevolent force. The curse let out one last, agonized cry before dissipating into nothingness, leaving behind only a faint echo.

The room fell silent, and Anna knew that the battle had been won. The curse that had haunted Willow Mansion for generations had been broken and the malevolent force had been vanquished.

As she stood in the moonlit ballroom, Anna felt a profound sense of accomplishment and relief. The spirits of the mansion gathered around her, their expressions filled with gratitude and happiness.

The curse that had once shrouded Willow Mansion in darkness had been lifted, and the mansion itself seemed to breathe a sigh of relief. The atmosphere shifted from one of oppression to one of serenity and tranquility.

Anna knew that her mission was complete and that she had rewritten the destiny of Willow Mansion. The spirits of Isabella, Samuel, Victoria, Eleanor, and Alexander were finally free, and the mansion's legacy had been transformed from one of tragedy to one of love and redemption.

With a sense of fulfillment, Anna bid farewell to the spirits of the mansion, knowing that their stories would endure as a testament to the enduring power of love, courage, and the ability to overcome even the darkest of curses.

Willow Mansion had been liberated from its haunted past, and Anna's journey had come to an end. As she left the ballroom, she couldn't help but feel a deep connection to the spirits and the history of the mansion. Her mission had been a testament to the extraordinary, a tale of love that had transcended time and death—a tale that would forever linger in the halls of Willow Mansion, waiting to be discovered by those who dared to enter its enigmatic embrace.

Chapter 18: The Unraveling Fate

With the curse of Willow Mansion finally broken, Anna's journey had come full circle. The mansion, once shrouded in darkness and haunted by malevolent forces, had been transformed into a place of peace and serenity. The spirits of Isabella, Samuel, Victoria, Eleanor, and Alexander were free, and their stories had been preserved as a testament to the enduring power of love and redemption.

As Anna continued her life outside the mansion, she couldn't help but feel a profound sense of fulfillment. Her mission had been a remarkable one—a journey of discovery, courage, and the unwavering belief in the ability to rewrite destiny.

But fate had one more surprise in store for Anna. One evening, as she was visiting the local historical society to share the history of Willow Mansion, she met a historian named Daniel. He was captivated by the stories of the mansion and its inhabitants, and he shared Anna's passion for preserving history.

As they spent more time together, Anna and Daniel's connection deepened. They found themselves drawn to each other, their shared interests and values creating a strong bond. It was a connection that felt fated, as though the spirits of Willow Mansion had played a hand in bringing them together.

As their romance blossomed, Anna realized that her own love story was mirroring the tales of love that she had uncovered within the mansion's walls. She and Daniel were united by a shared passion for history and a belief in the power of love to transcend time and adversity.

But Anna also knew that their love was a testament to the love stories of Isabella, Samuel, Victoria, Eleanor, and Alexander. Their spirits seemed to linger in the background, guiding Anna and Daniel as they embarked on their journey of love and discovery.

With each passing day, Anna and Daniel's love deepened, and they found themselves building a future together—a future that honored the spirits of Willow Mansion and celebrated the enduring power of love and redemption.

As they stood together in the moonlight one evening, Anna couldn't help but feel a sense of gratitude for the remarkable journey that had brought her to this moment. The curse had been broken, the spirits of the mansion had found their peace, and Anna had found her sense of purpose and belonging in the world.

Willow Mansion had been transformed from a place of darkness into a place of light and redemption, and Anna had played a pivotal role in its remarkable journey. As she and Daniel looked toward their future, they knew that their love would forever be intertwined with the stories of the past—a love that had been born in darkness but had emerged into the light, just like the love stories of Willow Mansion.

And so, Anna's journey had come to an end, but her legacy would endure as a testament to the enduring power of love, courage, and the belief in the ability to rewrite fate. Willow Mansion's history had been rewritten, and a new chapter had begun—one filled with love, hope, and the promise of a brighter future.

Chapter 19: The Forbidden Kiss

Anna and Daniel's love continued to deepen, their bond growing stronger with each passing day. Their connection was undeniable, and they found themselves drawn to one another in ways that felt almost otherworldly.

One warm summer evening, as they strolled through a nearby park, the moonlight casting a silvery glow on their surroundings, Anna and Daniel found themselves standing beneath a centuries-old willow tree. Its branches swayed gently in the breeze, and its leaves rustled with the secrets of time.

As they gazed up at the majestic tree, Anna couldn't help but feel a sense of connection to the willow tree in the mansion's garden, a place where Isabella and Samuel had once declared their love for each other. It was as though the spirits of the mansion were watching over them, blessing their love.

With a sense of reverence, Anna and Daniel approached the willow tree. Its branches formed a natural canopy, creating an intimate space beneath it. They stood facing each other, their hearts filled with a mixture of love and longing.

In that moment, they both felt a profound connection to the love stories of Willow Mansion—the forbidden love of Isabella and Samuel, the enduring love of Victoria and her lost family, and the shared dream of Eleanor and Alexander.

Anna and Daniel's love story, too, had faced its share of challenges. Society frowned upon their love, considering it a forbidden romance. But like the spirits of the mansion who had defied the curse, they had persevered in the face of adversity.

With a gentle, yet passionate gaze, Daniel reached out

to caress Anna's cheek. His touch sent shivers down her spine, and their eyes locked in a shared moment of longing. It was a moment that echoed the forbidden kisses and stolen glances of the past, a moment that celebrated their love despite the odds.

Unable to resist the pull of their emotions, Anna and Daniel leaned in closer. Their lips met in a kiss that was both tender and passionate, a kiss that spoke of love's ability to defy convention and transcend time.

Under the watchful branches of the willow tree, their love blossomed—a love that honored the spirits of Willow Mansion and celebrated the enduring power of love and redemption. It was a love that had been born in darkness but had emerged into the light, just like the love stories of the mansion.

As they finally pulled away from the kiss, their hearts beat in synchrony, and they knew that their love was a testament to the remarkable journey they had embarked upon. The spirits of Willow Mansion seemed to whisper their approval in the rustling leaves of the ancient willow tree.

Anna and Daniel's love story had become a part of the mansion's history, a continuation of the love and redemption that had unfolded within its walls. With a sense of gratitude and a deep connection to the past, they left the park hand in hand, knowing that their love was destined to endure—a love that had been blessed by the spirits of Willow Mansion and forged in the shadows of forbidden kisses.

Chapter 20: The Binding Spell

As Anna and Daniel's love story continued to flourish, they couldn't ignore the deep connection they felt to the spirits of Willow Mansion. The presence of Isabella, Samuel, Victoria, Eleanor, and Alexander seemed to linger in the background, as though they were guardians of love and redemption.

One evening, while researching the history of the mansion together, Anna stumbled upon an ancient spell—a binding spell that had the power to unite the spirits of the past with the living uniquely and profoundly. It was a spell that could strengthen the bond between the worlds of the living and the dead.

With the discovery of the binding spell, Anna and Daniel realized that they had the opportunity to forge an even deeper connection with the spirits of Willow Mansion. They believed that by performing the spell, they could honor the spirits and acknowledge the role they had played in shaping their own love story.

Anna and Daniel decided to conduct the binding spell in the very heart of Willow Mansion, in the grand ballroom where they had once confronted the curse. The room held a special significance, as it was a place where the spirits had found their peace.

They gathered the necessary ingredients—a vial of moonlit water, a sprig of willow leaves, and a lock of their hair, symbolizing their connection to the past and the present.

With candles flickering and the moonlight streaming in through the windows, Anna and Daniel began to recite the incantations of the binding spell. The room seemed to come alive with energy, and the atmosphere was charged with a sense of anticipation.

As the spell unfolded, they felt a gentle presence surrounding them—a presence that they knew to be the spirits of Willow Mansion. Isabella, Samuel, Victoria, Eleanor, and Alexander seemed to materialize in the room, their ethereal forms bathed in a soft, silvery light.

The spirits gazed at Anna and Daniel with smiles of approval, their eyes filled with warmth and gratitude. It was a moment of profound connection, a union between the living and the dead, and a celebration of the enduring power of love.

As the binding spell reached its conclusion, Anna and Daniel felt a sense of completeness, as though they had forged an unbreakable bond with the spirits of the mansion. The spirits, in turn, seemed to convey their blessings, as if they were guardians of love and redemption.

With the spell completed, Anna and Daniel knew that their love story had become even more intertwined with the history of Willow Mansion. They felt a deep sense of gratitude and a profound connection to the past, and they knew that their love had been enriched by the presence of the spirits.

As they left the grand ballroom hand in hand, Anna and Daniel couldn't help but smile at the knowledge that their love was a continuation of the remarkable love stories of Willow Mansion. They knew that their journey had come full circle and that their love had been blessed by the spirits of the past—a love that had been born in darkness but had emerged into the light, a love that celebrated the enduring power of love and redemption.

With a sense of purpose and a deep connection to the history of the mansion, they looked toward their future together, knowing that their love was destined to endure, just like the love stories that had unfolded within the walls of Willow Mansion.

Chapter 21: A Love Tested

Anna and Daniel's love had been strengthened by their connection to the spirits of Willow Mansion, but they soon faced a challenge that would put their relationship to the test.

One crisp autumn day, as they were exploring the mansion's gardens, they stumbled upon a hidden chamber they had not seen before. It was a chamber that had been untouched by time, and its walls were adorned with ancient symbols and mystical artifacts.

Curiosity piqued, and Anna and Daniel entered the chamber, unaware of the powerful magic it contained. As they ventured further inside, they were enveloped in a shimmering, ethereal light, and the room seemed to come alive with energy.

In the center of the chamber stood a mirror, similar to the one that had played a pivotal role in Eleanor and Alexander's love story. But this mirror was different—it was a portal to another realm, a realm of tests and trials that would challenge their love in ways they could never have imagined.

Anna and Daniel hesitated, unsure of what lay ahead, but their love and curiosity propelled them forward. As they gazed into the mirror, they were transported to a mystical realm where time and space seemed to twist and turn.

In this realm, they encountered a series of challenges designed to test the strength of their love. They faced obstacles that forced them to confront their deepest fears and insecurities, and they had to rely on their love and trust in each other to overcome each trial.

One challenge tested their ability to communicate and listen to each other, another challenged their ability to forgive and let go of past hurts, and yet another forced them to confront their weaknesses and vulnerabilities.

Throughout these trials, Anna and Daniel's love was put to the test, and they had to dig deep within themselves to find the strength to persevere. They leaned on each other for support, their love growing stronger with each challenge they conquered.

As they neared the final trial, they realized that the mystical realm was a reflection of their relationship—the ups and downs, the doubts and insecurities, and the unwavering love that had carried them through it all.

In the end, they emerged from the mystical realm with a newfound sense of clarity and a deeper understanding of their love. They knew that their relationship had been tested and had emerged stronger than ever, a love that had weathered the storms of doubt and uncertainty.

As they returned to the chamber in Willow Mansion, they felt a sense of gratitude for the challenges they had faced. Their love had been tested and had proven itself to be unbreakable, a love that could withstand anything that came their way.

With a renewed sense of purpose and a deeper connection to each other, Anna and Daniel left the hidden chamber hand in hand, knowing that their love had been tested and had emerged victorious. They looked toward their future together with confidence, knowing that their love was destined to endure, just like the love stories that had unfolded within the walls of Willow Mansion.

Chapter 22: The Final Confrontation

As Anna and Daniel emerged from the hidden chamber in Willow Mansion, they couldn't shake the feeling that their journey was coming to a climactic conclusion. The challenges they had faced in the mystical realm had strengthened their love, but they were left with a sense of unease, as though there was one final trial awaiting them.

Their intuition proved right when they received an ominous message—a message that seemed to materialize out of thin air. It was a cryptic warning, written in ancient symbols that spoke of a looming threat to the mansion and the spirits that resided within it.

The message hinted at a malevolent force that sought to reclaim its power and reassert control over the mansion. Anna and Daniel knew that they could not ignore this warning, and they realized that their love and the bond they had formed with the spirits of Willow Mansion would be put to the ultimate test.

With a sense of determination, they delved deeper into their research, uncovering clues that pointed to the existence of a hidden chamber beneath the mansion—one that held the key to the malevolent force's return. They believed that by confronting this force head-on, they could protect the mansion and the spirits that called it home.

Anna and Daniel's search led them to the mansion's basement, where they discovered a long-forgotten doorway concealed behind a tapestry. As they descended into the darkness, they were filled with a sense of foreboding, knowing that they were about to confront a powerful and vengeful entity.

In the depths of the hidden chamber, they found an altar adorned with ancient symbols and artifacts. It was a place of power, and at its center lay a dark, swirling void—a portal that seemed to pulse with malevolence.

As they approached the portal, the malevolent force revealed itself—a shape-shifting entity that seemed to feed on fear and despair. It taunted Anna and Daniel, promising to reclaim its hold on the mansion and destroy all that they held dear.

But Anna and Daniel were undeterred. They knew that their love and their connection to the spirits of Willow Mansion were their greatest strengths. With the spirits by their side, they confronted the malevolent force, using the knowledge they had gained from their journey and the binding spell they had performed.

A battle of wills ensued, as the malevolent force unleashed its dark powers, trying to overwhelm them with fear and doubt. But Anna and Daniel's love was a beacon of light that shone through the darkness, and they drew on the strength of the spirits and the enduring power of love and redemption.

With a final surge of determination, Anna and Daniel channeled their collective energy into a burst of light that engulfed the malevolent force. It let out a deafening cry of anguish and despair, and the portal collapsed, sealing the entity away once and for all.

As the darkness receded, Anna and Daniel stood in the chamber, victorious but exhausted. They knew that they had faced the ultimate test and had emerged triumphant, protecting the mansion and the spirits within it from the malevolent force's grip.

With a sense of relief and gratitude, they left the hidden chamber and ascended to the surface, where they were greeted by the spirits of Willow Mansion. Isabella, Samuel, Victoria, Eleanor, and Alexander smiled at them, their eyes filled with appreciation and approval.

Anna and Daniel had confronted the final threat to the mansion and had emerged victorious, their love and their bond with the spirits stronger than ever. They knew that their journey had come full circle and that their love was destined to endure, just like the love stories that had unfolded within the walls of Willow Mansion.

As they stood together in the moonlight, Anna and Daniel felt a profound sense of closure and fulfillment. Their love story was now an integral part of the mansion's history, a continuation of the love and redemption that had defined it for generations.

With a deep connection to the past and a brighter future ahead, they looked toward their life together with a renewed sense of purpose, knowing that their love was a testament to the enduring power of love, courage, and the belief in the ability to confront even the darkest of challenges.

Willow Mansion had been protected, and its legacy had been transformed from one of darkness to one of light. Anna and Daniel's love had played a pivotal role in this transformation, and they knew that their journey had been a remarkable one—a journey of love that had transcended time and adversity, a journey that celebrated the enduring power of love and redemption.

Chapter 23: Love's Sacrifice

As Anna and Daniel's love story continued to unfold, they found themselves facing a difficult decision—one that would test the depth of their love and their commitment to each other and the spirits of Willow Mansion.

In the months that followed their final confrontation with the malevolent force, they discovered that the mansion held a secret of immense importance. It was a secret that could either bring them closer together or drive them apart.

Hidden within the mansion's archives, they found a prophecy—a prophecy that spoke of a powerful bond between a mortal and a spirit, a bond that had the potential to reshape the destiny of both worlds. The prophecy hinted that this bond could only be fulfilled through a great sacrifice—one that would test the limits of love and devotion.

Anna and Daniel knew that they were the mortal and the spirit mentioned in the prophecy. Their love had transcended the boundaries between the living and the dead, and they had forged a unique connection with the spirits of Willow Mansion. But the prophecy also warned that fulfilling the bond would come at a great cost, one that could change the course of their lives forever.

As they contemplated the prophecy, Anna and Daniel faced a difficult choice. They could choose to fulfill the bond and embrace the sacrifice it required, or they could walk away from it and lead a more conventional life together.

The decision weighed heavily on their hearts. They knew that fulfilling the bond would mean leaving behind the world they had known and embarking on a journey into the realm of the spirits—a realm where time and existence were fluid and unpredictable.

But their love was unshakeable, and their connection to the spirits was a source of strength and purpose. They couldn't ignore the deep sense of destiny that had brought them together, and they couldn't turn their backs on the spirits who had become a part of their lives.

With a sense of resolve, Anna and Daniel made the difficult choice to fulfill the bond and embrace the sacrifice it required. They knew that their love was worth any cost, and they believed that their journey was destined to continue in the realm of the spirits.

As they prepared for the sacrifice, they felt a mixture of anticipation and trepidation. They knew that their lives were about to change in ways they could not fully comprehend, but they were willing to face the unknown together.

In the moonlit garden of Willow Mansion, they performed the ritual that would bind their destinies together. It was a moment of profound significance, a union between the mortal and the spirit, a testament to the enduring power of love and devotion.

As the ritual reached its culmination, a radiant light enveloped Anna and Daniel, and they felt themselves being transported into the realm of the spirits. They knew that their journey was far from over, but they also knew that their love would be their guiding light in this new and unfamiliar world.

With a sense of purpose and a deep connection to each other and the spirits, Anna and Daniel embraced the sacrifice and the destiny that awaited them. Their love had transcended time and existence, and they were ready to face whatever challenges lay ahead, knowing that their love was a testament to the enduring power of love and redemption—a love that had been born in darkness but had emerged into the light, a love that had rewritten the destiny of Willow Mansion and would continue to shape their remarkable journey.

Chapter 24: The Curse's End

Anna and Daniel found themselves in a realm that existed beyond the boundaries of time and space, a realm where the spirits of Willow Mansion resided. They had fulfilled the prophecy, and their love had brought them to this extraordinary place.

In this ethereal realm, they were greeted by the spirits—Isabella, Samuel, Victoria, Eleanor, and Alexander. Their spectral forms glowed with a soft, silvery light, and they welcomed Anna and Daniel with smiles of recognition and approval.

The spirits explained that the sacrifice they had made had fulfilled an ancient pact, one that had bound their destinies together. Anna had become a spirit herself, sharing the timeless existence of the spirits of Willow Mansion. Daniel, while still mortal, possessed a unique connection to this realm, allowing him to visit and interact with Anna whenever he wished.

The curse that had haunted the mansion for generations had finally come to an end. The malevolent force had been vanquished, and the spirits of the mansion were free to find peace and happiness in this realm of eternal twilight.

Anna and Daniel's love had rewritten the destiny of Willow Mansion, transforming it from a place of darkness to one of light and redemption. Their sacrifice had not only freed the spirits but had also united the worlds of the living and the dead in a way that had never been achieved before.

As Anna and Daniel settled into their new existence, they found joy in the company of the spirits and the shared memories of their time together. They explored the vast expanse of the realm, discovering hidden wonders and ancient mysteries.

The bond between Anna and Daniel remained as strong as ever, despite the challenges of their unique situation. Daniel continued to visit Anna in the realm of the spirits, and their love remained a source of strength and comfort.

Over time, they realized that their love had transcended the boundaries of mortality and eternity. It was a love that defied the constraints of time and space, a love that had rewritten the destiny of Willow Mansion and continued to shape their remarkable journey.

As they looked toward the endless horizon of their existence, Anna and Daniel knew that their love was destined to endure—a love that had been born in darkness but had emerged into the light, a love that celebrated the enduring power of love and redemption.

The curse had finally been lifted, and the mansion itself seemed to breathe a sigh of relief. The atmosphere shifted from one of oppression to one of serenity and tranquility.

Willow Mansion had been liberated from its haunted past, and Anna and Daniel's journey had come full circle. Their love story was now an integral part of the mansion's history, a continuation of the love and redemption that had defined it for generations.

With a sense of fulfillment and a deep connection to the spirits and the history of the mansion, they looked toward their eternal future together, knowing that their love was destined to endure, just like the love stories that had unfolded within the walls of Willow Mansion.

And so, in the realm of spirits and eternal twilight, Anna and Daniel's love story continued as a testament to the enduring power of love and the belief in the ability to overcome even the darkest of curses—a love that would forever linger in the timeless embrace of Willow Mansion, waiting to be discovered by those who dared to enter its enigmatic world.

Chapter 25: A New Beginning

In the realm beyond time and space, Anna and Daniel's love story had entered a new phase—one that embraced the boundless possibilities of eternity. Their journey had taken them from the mortal realm to the realm of spirits, and now they stood at the threshold of a new beginning.

With each passing day, Anna and Daniel explored the mysteries of their newfound existence. They wandered through the timeless landscapes of the spirit realm, where forests of ancient trees whispered secrets of the past, and ethereal rivers flowed with memories from distant ages.

The spirits of Willow Mansion were their constant companions, guiding them through the vast expanse of their new world. Isabella, Samuel, Victoria, Eleanor, and Alexander shared their wisdom and stories, allowing Anna and Daniel to connect with the rich history of the mansion in ways they had never imagined.

But amid the wonder of their new life, Anna and Daniel could not forget their roots in the mortal world. They yearned to share the beauty of the spirit realm with those they had left behind, and so they devised a plan to bridge the gap between the living and the dead.

Using their unique connection to both realms, Anna and Daniel became messengers of love and hope. They visited the dreams of the living, leaving behind glimpses of the enchanting spirit realm, inspiring creativity, and planting the seeds of courage and love.

Their presence in the dreams of the living brought comfort and solace to those who had lost loved ones, allowing them to feel a connection to the world beyond. Anna and Daniel's love became a beacon of light in the darkness, a reminder that love transcended the boundaries of life and death.

As they continued their mission, Anna and Daniel discovered that the spirit realm held its own set of challenges and mysteries. They encountered ancient guardians, unearthed forgotten legends, and delved into the depths of their souls, all while nurturing their enduring love.

The spirit realm was a place of endless discovery, where time flowed differently, and existence was both timeless and ever-changing. Anna and Daniel embraced the adventure, knowing that their love was the guiding star in this uncharted territory.

And so, in the realm beyond time and space, Anna and Daniel's love story continued—a story of love, courage, and the enduring belief in the ability to bridge the gap between the living and the dead. Their journey was a testament to the enduring power of love and redemption, a journey that celebrated the boundless possibilities of eternity.

As they stood together in the eternal twilight of the spirit realm, Anna and Daniel knew that their love was destined to endure, just like the love stories that had unfolded within the walls of Willow Mansion. They were messengers of love, guiding spirits of hope, and guardians of a new beginning—a beginning that celebrated the enduring legacy of love and the infinite possibilities of eternity.

Chapter 26: Love Reborn

In the boundless realm beyond time and space, Anna and Daniel's love had blossomed into something even more profound—a love that transcended the limits of both mortality and eternity. Their journey had taken them to the farthest reaches of existence, and they had discovered that love was the thread that connected all worlds.

As they continued to explore the spirit realm, Anna and Daniel encountered souls from various ages and walks of life. They shared stories, experiences, and wisdom, forging connections with spirits who had traversed the boundaries of time alongside them.

One fateful encounter brought them face to face with a soul whose story uniquely touched their hearts. It was the spirit of a young woman named Amelia, who had lived in a different era but whose love story had been tragically cut short. Her spirit resonated with Anna and Daniel, and they felt an immediate connection.

Amelia's tale was one of unfulfilled love—a love that had been thwarted by circumstance and time. She had longed to experience the depth of love and devotion that Anna and Daniel shared, but her journey had been fraught with obstacles and heartbreak.

Touched by Amelia's story, Anna and Daniel resolved to help her find the love and happiness she had been denied in life. They believed that their unique position in the spirit realm allowed them to offer guidance and support to souls like Amelia, helping them rewrite their destinies.

Together, they embarked on a quest to reunite Amelia with her lost love, a journey that would test the boundaries of their love and the power of redemption. Guided by the spirits of Willow Mansion and fueled by their unwavering belief in the transformative power of love, they set out to rewrite the story of Amelia's heart.

Their journey took them through the tapestries of time, as they visited different eras and witnessed the beauty and complexity of human love. Along the way, they encountered challenges and obstacles that tested their resolve, but their love remained a beacon of hope and determination.

As they unraveled the threads of Amelia's story, they discovered that love was not bound by the constraints of time or mortality. It was a force that could transcend the ages, a force that could rewrite the destiny of even the most star-crossed souls.

With each step of their journey, Anna and Daniel brought Amelia closer to her lost love, helping her heal the wounds of the past and embrace the love she had always yearned for. Their efforts were rewarded with the joyous reunion of two souls who had been separated by time but were destined to be together.

Amelia's love story became a testament to the enduring power of love and the belief in the ability to rewrite destiny. As she and her lost love embraced in the spirit realm, their happiness radiated like a beacon of light, a love reborn and renewed.

Anna and Daniel's love had grown even deeper through their mission of love and redemption. They realized that their journey in the spirit realm was not just about their own love story but also about the countless souls they could touch and inspire with the transformative power of love.

As they continued their exploration of the boundless realm, Anna and Daniel knew that their love was destined to endure, just like the love stories that had unfolded within the walls of Willow Mansion. Love, they had learned, was a force that could transcend all boundaries and ignite the hearts of souls across time and eternity—a force that could rewrite destinies and offer the promise of a love reborn.

Chapter 27: The Ghostly Woman's Farewell

As Anna, Daniel, and the spirits of Willow Mansion continued their timeless journey through the spirit realm, a bittersweet chapter awaited them—one that would both celebrate the enduring power of love and acknowledge the inevitability of change.

Amelia, the spirit whose love story they had helped rewrite, had found the happiness and closure she had longed for. Her reunion with her lost love had been a joyous and transformative experience, one that had filled the spirit realm with a radiant light of love reborn.

Amelia's newfound happiness had a profound impact on Anna and Daniel. They realized that their mission to guide and support souls like Amelia had touched many lives in the spirit realm, and their love had been a catalyst for profound transformations.

However, with happiness also came the realization that it was time for Amelia to move on to the next stage of her spiritual journey. She had found the love and closure she had sought, and her spirit was ready to transition to a higher plane of existence.

One evening, in the moonlit garden of the spirit realm, Anna, Daniel, and the spirits of Willow Mansion gathered to bid farewell to Amelia. She stood before them, her ethereal form radiant with love and gratitude.

Amelia expressed her profound thanks to Anna and Daniel for helping her rewrite her destiny and find the love that had eluded her in life. Her words were filled with warmth and appreciation, and she spoke of the transformative power of their love and the enduring bond they had formed.

Tears of both joy and sadness glistened in Anna and Daniel's eyes as they embraced Amelia one last time. They knew that her departure marked a significant moment in their journey—a moment that celebrated the beauty of love and the inevitability of change.

Amelia's farewell was a reminder that the spirit realm was a place of transition and transformation, where souls embarked on their unique journeys of growth and enlightenment. Her departure symbolized the eternal cycle of existence, where love remained a constant, even as souls moved on to new experiences and adventures.

As Amelia's spirit ascended to a higher plane of existence, she left behind a trail of shimmering stardust that illuminated the night sky of the spirit realm. Her departure was a testament to the enduring power of love and the belief in the ability to find happiness and fulfillment, even in the afterlife.

Anna, Daniel, and the spirits of Willow Mansion watched as Amelia's light faded into the infinite expanse of the spirit realm. Her departure left them with a sense of both loss and hope—a recognition that love was an eternal force that bound all souls together, even as they embarked on their journeys.

With renewed purpose and a deeper understanding of the ever-changing nature of existence, Anna and Daniel continued their exploration of the spirit realm. They knew that their journey was far from over and that their love would remain a guiding light in the boundless realm beyond time and space.

As they stood in the moonlit garden, surrounded by the spirits of Willow Mansion, they felt a sense of gratitude for the profound experiences and transformations they had witnessed. Love, they knew, was the constant

thread that connected all souls, and their journey celebrated the enduring power of love and the belief in the ability to shape destinies and offer the promise of a love that transcended even the boundaries of the spirit realm.

Chapter 28: Forever and Always

In the ethereal realm beyond time and space, Anna and Daniel's love story had evolved into a timeless tapestry of shared experiences, adventures, and boundless devotion. They had journeyed through the spirit realm, rewriting destinies and touching the hearts of countless souls, all while deepening their love and connection.

As they continued to explore the spirit realm, they discovered that it was a place where memories held a unique power. Memories were like stars that lit up the darkness, illuminating the past and connecting it to the present.

One evening, while wandering through the ancient forests of the spirit realm, Anna and Daniel stumbled upon a grove of shimmering trees. Each tree was adorned with radiant orbs of light that pulsed with the energy of memories.

Intrigued by this enchanting sight, they approached one of the luminous orbs and reached out to touch it. As their fingers made contact, they were instantly transported into a memory—a memory that was both their own and yet not their own.

They found themselves reliving a moment from their past, one of the many beautiful moments they had shared in their mortal lives. It was a memory of a moonlit dance in the garden of Willow Mansion, a dance that solidified their love and set their destiny in motion.

The memory was vivid and enchanting, and they could feel the warmth of each other's hands, hear the soft music playing in the background, and see the love reflected in each other's eyes. It was a moment frozen in time, a testament to the enduring power of their love.

As they embraced the memory, they realized that the grove of shimmering trees held countless memories from their lives together—moments of joy, laughter, and love. Each memory was a treasure, a reminder of the beautiful journey they had embarked upon.

With each memory they explored, Anna and Daniel's love deepened even further. They saw their love from different perspectives, reliving moments of tenderness, passion, and shared dreams. It was as if they were experiencing their love anew, with a profound appreciation for the depth of their connection.

But amid the beauty of these memories, they also encountered moments of challenge and adversity. They saw the times when their love had been tested when doubts had crept in, and when they had leaned on each other for strength and support. These memories served as a reminder that their love had grown stronger through the trials they had faced together.

As they continued to explore the grove of memories, Anna and Daniel realized that their love was an intricate tapestry woven from countless threads of shared experiences and emotions. It was a tapestry that spanned both mortal and immortal realms, a tapestry that celebrated the enduring power of love.

With a sense of wonder and gratitude, Anna and Daniel knew that their love was destined to endure, not only in the present but also in the memories they had created together. Their journey through the spirit realm had deepened their connection to each other and the boundless expanse of existence.

As they stood in the grove of shimmering trees, surrounded by the memories of their love, they made a silent vow to cherish each moment and continue their exploration of the spirit realm. Their love was a journey without end, a journey filled with the promise of forever and always—a journey that celebrated the enduring power of love and the belief in the ability to create lasting memories that would transcend even the boundaries of time and eternity.

Chapter 29: An Eternal Bond

Anna and Daniel's journey through the spirit realm led them to discover the profound interconnectedness of all souls and the enduring power of love. As they continued their exploration, they encountered a revelation that would forever change the course of their own love story.

One serene evening, while strolling along the banks of an otherworldly river, Anna and Daniel came across a shimmering pool of water that seemed to reflect the very essence of existence. They approached the pool, drawn by its mesmerizing beauty, and gazed into its depths.

To their astonishment, the pool revealed a vision of their own love story, from its inception in the mortal realm to their adventures in the spirit realm. It was a vivid and moving portrayal of their journey, and they watched with awe as their love unfolded before them.

But what was even more remarkable was that they saw glimpses of other souls intertwined with their own story. They saw the spirits of Willow Mansion, Isabella, Samuel, Victoria, Eleanor, and Alexander, who had played a pivotal role in their journey. They saw the souls they had encountered along the way, including Amelia, whose love story they had helped rewrite.

As they continued to watch, they realized that the pool was showing them the interconnected web of love that bound all souls together. Their own love story was just one thread in this vast tapestry, and it was woven together with the stories of countless other souls they had touched and transformed.

Anna and Daniel understood that their journey had not only been about their love but also about the love they had shared with others, the love they had inspired and nurtured. It was a love that transcended the boundaries of time and existence, a love that connected them to the spirits of Willow Mansion and the souls they had encountered along the way.

With this profound revelation, Anna and Daniel felt a sense of purpose and responsibility. They realized that their love had the power to uplift and transform not only their own lives but also the lives of others. They were guardians of a love that was boundless and eternal, a love that celebrated the interconnectedness of all souls.

As they continued their journey, they sought out other souls in need of guidance and support. They shared their wisdom, offered solace to the grieving, and helped souls find their paths to love and redemption. Their mission had expanded beyond their own love story, encompassing the greater tapestry of love that connected all souls in the spirit realm.

With each soul they touched, Anna and Daniel felt their love grow even deeper. They realized that their journey was not just a personal one but a universal one—a journey that celebrated the eternal bond of love that connected all souls, a bond that transcended the boundaries of time and space.

In the realm beyond time and space, Anna and Daniel's love story had evolved into a profound and eternal bond—a bond that celebrated the interconnectedness of all souls, a bond that embraced the enduring power of love and the belief in the ability to uplift and transform the lives of others.

As they stood by the shimmering pool, gazing into its depths, they knew that their love was destined to endure, not just in their hearts but in the hearts of all the souls they had touched. Their journey had become a testament to the universal and eternal nature of love—an eternal bond that celebrated the interconnected web of love that connected all souls in the boundless expanse of existence.

Chapter 30: Love Beyond the Grave

Anna and Daniel's journey through the spirit realm led them to profound revelations about the enduring power of love and the interconnectedness of all souls. They had embraced their role as guardians of love, helping souls find redemption and transformation. Yet, their journey was far from over, and a final revelation awaited them—one that would illuminate the ultimate truth about their love.

One moonlit night, as they wandered through the ever-changing landscapes of the spirit realm, they found themselves standing before a grand and ancient oak tree. Its branches reached toward the starlit sky, and its roots delved deep into the soil of the spirit realm, connecting it to the memories of countless souls.

Anna and Daniel felt drawn to the tree, sensing that it held a profound secret. As they approached, the tree's bark began to shimmer, revealing a series of intricate carvings that depicted the stories of love and redemption from across the ages.

They realized that the tree was a living chronicle of the spirit realm, a repository of the memories, experiences, and love stories of all who had passed through its realm. It was a testament to the enduring nature of existence, where love continued to thrive beyond the confines of mortality.

As they touched the carvings, they were transported into the memories of souls who had once walked the mortal world. They saw love stories that had transcended time and space, where love had endured even in the face of death.

They witnessed the tale of a devoted couple who had been separated by tragedy but had found each other in the afterlife, where their love had been rekindled in an eternal embrace. They saw the love of a parent and child, whose bond had remained unbroken even after they had crossed into the spirit realm.

But what moved them the most were the stories of love that had transcended the boundaries between the living and the dead. They saw souls who had returned from the afterlife to guide and protect their loved ones, offering comfort and solace in times of need.

It was in these stories that Anna and Daniel discovered the ultimate truth about their love. Their journey had not only been a celebration of love's enduring power but also a testament to the belief that love could thrive beyond the grave.

They realized that their love was not bound by the limitations of mortality or the spirit realm. It was a love that transcended all boundaries, a love
that would endure for all eternity.

With this profound revelation, Anna and Daniel felt a sense of peace and completeness. They understood that their love was a force that had the power to transcend even death itself, a force that would continue to connect their souls in the boundless expanse of existence.

As they stood before the grand oak tree, they made a silent vow to cherish their love for all eternity, knowing that it was a love that defied all boundaries and celebrated the ultimate truth—that love, in its purest form, was a force that could endure beyond the grave.

Their journey through the spirit realm had come full circle, and they had discovered the deepest truth of all—that love, in its most profound and enduring form, was a love beyond the grave.

Chapter 1: Moonlit Encounter Ensnared by the Werewolf's Heart: A Love in the Night

The night was bathed in the silvery glow of a full moon, casting an ethereal light over the dense forest. Emily had always found solace in the woods near her family's cabin, but tonight, there was an undeniable magic in the air. A gentle breeze whispered through the trees, carrying with it the sweet scent of pine and earth.

Emily's footsteps crunched softly on the forest floor as she wandered deeper into the woods. Her heart was heavy with the weight of her secrets and worries. She had come here to escape the pressures of her everyday life, to lose herself in the embrace of nature.

As she walked, Emily's keen eyes caught a flash of movement in the underbrush. Startled, she froze her senses on high alert. Her heart quickened, and her hand instinctively reached for the pocket knife she always carried. She had heard tales of wild animals in these woods, and she wasn't about to become prey.

The rustling grew louder and closer. Emily's breath caught in her throat as she cautiously approached the source of the sound. There, hidden in the shadows, lay a wounded wolf. Its fur was matted with dirt and blood, and its eyes held a mix of fear and pain.

Emily's heart went out to the creature. She knelt, her fear giving way to compassion. "It's okay," she whispered soothingly, extending a trembling hand toward the injured animal. "I won't hurt you."

The wolf's eyes locked onto Emily's, and for a moment, time seemed to stand still. In those eyes, she saw not just the wildness of a beast but the soul of a sentient being. It was as if they were connected by an invisible thread of understanding.

With great care, Emily examined the wolf's injuries. She found a deep gash on its side that oozed blood. Without hesitation, she tore a piece of her shirt to fashion a makeshift bandage. The wolf watched her every move, its trust slowly growing.

As Emily worked, the forest seemed to hold its breath. The moon's radiant glow enveloped them, casting an otherworldly aura around the scene. When she had finished tending to the wolf's wound, she met its gaze once more. It was then that she saw a flicker of something extraordinary in its eyes.

With a shiver of realization, Emily took a step back, her heart pounding. Could it be? Could this wolf, wounded and vulnerable, be more than it seemed? A legend whispered in her mind—a legend of creatures who transformed under the light of the full moon, of werewolves.

As if in response to her thoughts, the wounded wolf's body began to tremble. Emily watched in awe as the transformation unfolded before her eyes. The wolf's form contorted and shifted until a man now stood before her, naked and vulnerable.

Stunned and speechless, Emily stared at the man who had emerged from the wolf's body. He had a rugged, yet undeniably handsome, appearance, with hair as dark as the night and eyes that held a hint of mystery. The realization struck her like a thunderbolt: the wolf, this man, was a werewolf.

In the silence of the moonlit forest, the two of them stood as strangers bound by an extraordinary encounter. Emily's heart raced with a mixture of fear and fascination. Little did she know that this chance meeting with a wounded werewolf would set in motion a love story that would defy the boundaries of the ordinary world and take her on an extraordinary journey into the heart of the night.

Chapter 2: A Secret Revealed

The moon continued to cast its silvery glow upon the forest, illuminating the tension that hung between Emily and the man who had once been a wounded wolf. She swallowed hard, her mind racing as she grappled with the astonishing truth that stood before her.

The man, whose name she did not yet know, regarded her with a mixture of vulnerability and wariness. He spoke in a voice that carried a hint of both humility and pride. "My name is Ethan," he began, his eyes never leaving Emily's. "I am a werewolf."

Emily's heart raced, and her breath caught in her throat. She had heard tales of supernatural creatures, but she had never imagined she would encounter one, let alone fall into the company of a werewolf. Questions tumbled through her mind like leaves caught in a whirlwind.

Ethan seemed to sense her fear and confusion. With a gentle, reassuring smile, he continued, "I mean you no harm, Emily. You saved my life tonight."

The weight of his words sank in. Emily had indeed saved his life, and in doing so, she had stumbled upon a world she could barely comprehend. She found her voice, though it trembled as she spoke. "I didn't know... I didn't know werewolves were real."

Ethan nodded, his eyes softening. "We are very real, though we remain hidden from most of the world. Our existence is a closely guarded secret."

Emily took a step closer to him, the fear slowly giving way to curiosity. "Why did you reveal yourself to me?"

Ethan hesitated, his gaze dropping to the forest floor. "I don't fully understand it myself," he admitted. "But something about you drew me in. Your kindness, your bravery—it touched something deep within me. I couldn't let you be frightened or harmed because of what I am."

As Emily listened to his words, a warmth spread through her chest. Despite the fear and uncertainty that still lingered, she couldn't deny the connection that had formed between them. She had saved a life tonight, and in return, she had been shown a secret world beyond her wildest dreams.

"I won't tell anyone about you," Emily promised, her voice firm with determination. "Your secret is safe with me."

Ethan's gratitude shone in his eyes. "Thank you, Emily. That means more to me than you can know."

Their conversation continued late into the night, as they sat beneath the canopy of trees, their voices a soft exchange in the moonlight. Emily learned about the complexities of Ethan's life as a werewolf—the challenges of transformation, the bonds of his pack, and the secrecy that shrouded their existence.

In turn, she shared her struggles, her dreams, and the reasons she had sought solace in the forest that night. With each passing moment, their connection deepened, and the lines that separated their worlds blurred.

As the first light of dawn began to paint the eastern sky, Emily and Ethan realized that they had forged a bond that defied the ordinary. A love story had begun, one that would challenge the boundaries of their worlds and ignite a passion that would burn brighter than the moon itself.

Their love had been ensnared by the night, and they were about to embark on a journey where secrets, dangers, and the strength of their hearts would be put to the ultimate test.

Chapter 3: The Unlikely Pair

Days turned into weeks, and Emily and Ethan's bond deepened. They continued to meet in the moonlit forest, sharing secrets, dreams, and stories beneath the watchful gaze of the full moon. Despite the challenges that lay ahead, their connection grew stronger with each passing night.

Ethan introduced Emily to the hidden beauty of the forest, revealing its mysteries and enchantments. Together, they explored forgotten paths, discovered hidden waterfalls, and marveled at the flora and fauna that thrived in the heart of the woods.

One evening, as they sat by a tranquil, moonlit pond, Emily broke the silence that had settled between them. "Ethan," she began, her voice soft and contemplative, "what is it like to be a werewolf?"

Ethan regarded her with a thoughtful expression, his eyes reflecting the moon's gentle glow. "It's a life of contrasts," he said. "The transformation, the strength, and the heightened senses are incredible, but they come with their own set of challenges. We must be vigilant during the full moon to ensure we do not harm others."

Emily nodded, absorbing his words. "And your pack? Are they like family to you?"

Ethan's gaze turned distant for a moment. "Yes," he replied, a note of sadness in his voice. "We are bound by a deep connection. But it's not always easy. There are conflicts, rivalries, and disagreements, just like any family."

Emily could sense the weight of his responsibilities as a member of the pack. She reached out and gently placed her hand on his, offering silent support. In that simple gesture, their bond deepened even further.

As the weeks passed, Emily introduced Ethan to her world. She took him to the nearby town, where they ventured cautiously, hidden beneath the cover of darkness. They shared ice cream at a local parlor and danced beneath the stars at a deserted fairground, their laughter ringing through the night.

Their love story was a delicate dance between two worlds—one filled with the enchantment of the forest, the other with the simplicity of everyday life. Emily marveled at the juxtaposition of it all, realizing that she had fallen for a man who was as extraordinary as he was humble.

One moonlit night, as Emily and Ethan sat side by side beneath their favorite oak tree, he turned to her, his eyes filled with a mixture of warmth and longing. "Emily," he began, his voice soft as a whisper, "I never imagined that I would find someone like you."

Emily's heart skipped a beat as she met his gaze. "And I never thought I'd meet a werewolf in the woods," she replied with a teasing smile.

Ethan chuckled, the sound like music in the night. "You are a remarkable woman, Emily. You've shown me kindness and acceptance when I least expected it."

She leaned closer, her hand finding his. "And you've shown me a world of wonder and love that I never knew existed."

Their lips met in a tender kiss beneath the moon's watchful eye. At that moment, surrounded by the magic of the night, Emily and Ethan realized that their love was something extraordinary—a love that defied the boundaries of their worlds, a

love that had been kindled in the moonlight, and a love that was destined to endure the trials that lay ahead.

Chapter 4: A Forbidden Love

As Emily and Ethan's love deepened, so did the challenges they faced. The world they inhabited was divided by an unspoken boundary—an unyielding line between the human and supernatural realms. Their love, while passionate and true, was considered forbidden by the norms of both worlds.

The news of their blossoming relationship had spread within the werewolf community, and not all members of Ethan's pack approved. Traditionalists argued that a human-werewolf relationship was not only unwise but dangerous. They feared it could expose their secret and endanger their existence.

In the human world, Emily's family had grown increasingly concerned about her absences and secretive behavior. Her father, John, had noticed the change in her and couldn't ignore the warning signs. He decided it was time to confront Emily about her newfound connection.

One evening, after Emily returned home from a night in the forest with Ethan, her father sat her down in the cozy living room of their cabin. The crackling fire provided a warm backdrop to their serious conversation.

"Emily," John began, his voice filled with worry, "I've noticed that you've been spending a lot of time away from home lately, especially during the full moon. You've been distant and secretive, and I can't help but be concerned."

Emily hesitated, torn between her love for Ethan and her loyalty to her family. "Dad, there's something I need to tell you," she finally admitted. "I've met someone, someone who's... different. His name is Ethan, and he's not like anyone I've ever known."

John's brows furrowed as he listened. "Different how?"

Emily took a deep breath, her heart heavy with the weight of her secret. "Ethan is a werewolf, Dad."

John's eyes widened in shock, and he struggled to process the revelation. "A werewolf? Emily, you can't be serious."

Tears welled up in Emily's eyes as she nodded. "I wish it weren't true, Dad, but it is. I didn't choose to fall in love with him; it just happened."

John's concern turned to anger, and he clenched his fists in frustration. "Emily, you have to understand how dangerous this is. If anyone in the town finds out, it could put not only our family but the entire community at risk. We need to put an end to this before it goes any further."

Emily's heart sank, torn between her love for Ethan and her family's safety. She knew her father was right, but the thought of ending her relationship with Ethan felt like tearing her heart in two.

Meanwhile, in the werewolf community, Ethan faced similar challenges. Some pack members were openly hostile to his relationship with a human, fearing that it would bring unwanted attention to their kind. The tensions within the pack began to grow, threatening to tear it apart.

As Emily and Ethan navigated the treacherous waters of their forbidden love, they found themselves at a crossroads. Their love was undeniable, but the world around them seemed determined to keep them apart. In the face of societal prejudices, family concerns, and pack dynamics, they had to decide whether their love was worth the sacrifices they would have to make.

Chapter 5: Danger in the Night

The tension between Emily's desire to be with Ethan and her family's concerns continued to escalate. Her father, John, was adamant about ending her relationship with the werewolf, convinced that it posed a grave danger to their family and the entire community.

One fateful night, as Emily prepared to leave for another secret meeting with Ethan, John confronted her once more. His eyes were filled with a mix of anger, fear, and determination.

"Emily," he implored, "I can't let you go to him tonight. It's too dangerous."

Emily's heart ached as she gazed into her father's eyes, torn between her love for Ethan and her loyalty to her family. "Dad, I love him. I can't just abandon him."

John's frustration reached its breaking point. "Emily, you don't understand what's at stake. If the townspeople discover his true nature, there will be chaos. Our family will be ostracized, and we'll lose everything we've built here."

Tears welled up in Emily's eyes as she considered the painful choice before her. She knew her father was right, but the thought of leaving Ethan behind felt like a betrayal of her heart.

In the heart of the forest, Ethan was grappling with challenges of his own. The tensions within his pack had grown even more volatile. Some pack members openly accused him of putting their secrecy at risk with his involvement with a human. Others, however, saw the depth of his love for Emily and supported him.

One night, as the full moon bathed the forest in its luminous glow, a rival pack from a neighboring territory threatened Ethan's pack. Their leader, a formidable werewolf named Victor, had long harbored animosity toward Ethan's pack and saw their vulnerability as an opportunity for power.

Victor and his pack ambushed Ethan's group, sparking a violent confrontation under the moonlit canopy. Emily's heart raced as she sensed that something was amiss. She had a deep connection to Ethan, and she knew when he was in danger.

Driven by love and concern, Emily ventured into the forest despite her father's warnings. She was determined to find Ethan and ensure his safety. Little did she know that danger lurked in the shadows, waiting to ensnare them both.

As Emily ventured deeper into the forest, she stumbled upon the aftermath of the brutal clash between the rival werewolf packs. The scene was chaotic, with wounded wolves and signs of the fierce battle that had taken place. Panic surged through her as she realized the danger Ethan was in.

Finally, she spotted him—bruised and battered but still standing, his eyes filled with a determination to protect his pack. Emily rushed to his side, her heart aching at the sight of his injuries.

"Ethan!" she cried, throwing her arms around him. "Are you okay?"

He held her tightly, his voice strained with pain. "I'm alive, Emily. But this isn't over. Victor won't stop until he's taken control of our pack."

As they clung to each other in the moonlit forest, Emily and Ethan knew that their love had led them into the heart of danger. Their forbidden romance had brought them to a crossroads where they had to face the consequences of their choices and the threats that loomed on the horizon.

Chapter 6: Under the Moonlight

The moon hung in the sky, casting its ethereal glow upon Emily and Ethan as they stood together in the aftermath of the violent clash between the rival werewolf packs. Emily's heart ached as she took in the sight of Ethan's battered form, his eyes reflecting a mix of pain and determination.

With gentle hands, Emily helped Ethan to a fallen log, and they sat down, their shoulders touching as they sought solace in each other's presence. The forest was eerily silent after the chaos as if nature itself held its breath in anticipation of what would come next.

"Ethan, we have to find a way to stop Victor," Emily said, her voice filled with resolve. "We can't let him destroy your pack or harm anyone else."

Ethan nodded, his jaw clenched in determination. "You're right, Emily. We can't let him continue unchecked. But we must be careful. Victor is powerful and ruthless."

Their hands found each other, fingers intertwining under the moonlit canopy. At that moment, they made a silent promise to stand together against the impending threat, no matter the cost.

As the days passed, Emily and Ethan worked tirelessly to gather information about Victor's plans. They ventured deep into the heart of the forest, consulting with trusted members of Ethan's pack and devising a strategy to confront the rival werewolves.

Under the moonlight, their connection seemed to strengthen, and their love deepened with every stolen moment they spent together. The forest became their sanctuary, a place where they could escape the turmoil of their respective worlds and find solace in each other's arms.

One night, as they lay beneath the starry sky, their fingers tracing patterns on each other's skin, Emily whispered, "I love you, Ethan. No matter what happens, remember that."

Ethan turned to her, his eyes filled with a depth of emotion that left her breathless. "And I love you, Emily. You are my anchor in this chaotic world."

Their lips met in a passionate kiss, sealing their love beneath the moonlight. In that stolen moment, they found strength and courage, knowing that they could face whatever challenges lay ahead as long as they had each other.

The night of reckoning with Victor drew near, and Emily and Ethan knew that their love had been tested and forged in the crucible of danger. As they stood on the precipice of a battle that would determine the fate of their pack and their love, they were determined to face it together, unyielding in their commitment to each other and the enduring power of their love under the moonlight.

Chapter 7: Family Matters

The looming confrontation with Victor and the rival werewolf pack weighed heavily on Emily and Ethan's hearts. As they made their preparations in the moonlit forest, their bond grew stronger, but they also faced challenges from those closest to them—Emily's family and Ethan's pack.

Emily's father, John, had become increasingly adamant about keeping her away from Ethan. He couldn't shake the fear that their forbidden love would lead to catastrophe. One evening, he gathered the family for a heart-to-heart discussion.

"Emily," John began, his voice trembling with concern, "I can't stand by and watch you risk your life for this... this relationship with Ethan. It's tearing our family apart, and I'm afraid it will bring harm to us all."

Emily's mother, Sarah, placed a comforting hand on her daughter's shoulder. "John, we understand your worries, but we also see how much Emily cares for him. Perhaps we should try to find a way to ensure her safety while allowing her to make her own choices."

Emily's younger brother, Jacob, chimed in, "Dad, we can't force Emily to do something she doesn't want to do. Maybe we should trust her judgment."

John sighed, torn between his protective instincts and his love for his daughter. "I just don't want to lose her," he admitted.

Emily, her heart heavy with the burden of her family's concerns, said, "Dad, I love you, and I appreciate your concern. But I can't turn my back on Ethan when he needs me the most. I promise to be cautious and do everything I can to keep us all safe."

John reluctantly nodded, realizing that he couldn't stand in the way of his daughter's determination. The family's discussion ended with a sense of uneasy compromise, but Emily knew that the road ahead would not be easy.

In the werewolf community, Ethan faced his challenges. While some members of his pack supported his love for Emily, others remained deeply skeptical. Pack dynamics had become increasingly strained, with tensions threatening to divide the group.

One night, as Ethan sought the counsel of his pack's elder, Clara, he shared his concerns. "Clara, I don't know how to bridge the divide within our pack. Victor is still a looming threat, and I fear that our internal conflicts will only weaken us further."

Clara regarded him with wisdom in her eyes. "Ethan, love has a power of its own. It can heal wounds and bridge divides if you let it. You must find a way to unite your pack behind the strength of your love for Emily. Only then can you face Victor together."

Ethan nodded, realizing that he needed to be a beacon of unity and hope for his pack. With Clara's guidance, he began the arduous task of mending the rifts within his pack and convincing them that love, even between a werewolf and a human, could be a source of strength.

As the days passed, Emily and Ethan continued to navigate the challenges posed by their families and their respective worlds. They drew strength from their love, knowing that it was the one constant in a world filled with uncertainty.

The night of the final confrontation with Victor drew nearer, and Emily and Ethan were determined to face it together, with their families and pack members by their side. They had learned that love could be a powerful force for change and unity, and they were willing to fight for a future where love transcended the boundaries of their worlds.

Chapter 8: The Pack's Approval

In the days leading up to the inevitable clash with Victor's rival werewolf pack, Ethan devoted himself to uniting his pack behind the strength of his love for Emily. It was a challenging endeavor, as the tensions within the pack had run deep for years.

Ethan called for a meeting with his fellow pack members in a secluded clearing beneath the full moon. His voice, filled with conviction, resonated through the night as he spoke of love, unity, and the importance of embracing change.

"I understand that my relationship with Emily has caused fear and uncertainty among some of you," Ethan began, his eyes locking with those of his pack members. "But I want you to know that love can be a source of strength, not weakness. It has given me the determination to protect our pack and the woman I love."

One by one, pack members voiced their concerns, their skepticism, and their fears. They worried that Emily's presence would expose them to danger, but Ethan patiently listened to each voice, acknowledging their fears.

Finally, an elder pack member named Samuel spoke up. "Ethan, while we may not fully understand your love for Emily, we see the sincerity in your eyes. We have been divided for too long, and perhaps it's time we embrace change."

Ethan's heart swelled with hope as he realized that his pack was slowly coming to accept his relationship with Emily. He knew that their unity was crucial if they were to stand a chance against Victor's pack.

In the human world, Emily had also been working tirelessly to ease her family's concerns. She had introduced Ethan to her family, hoping that seeing the sincerity of their love would help alleviate some of their fears.

One evening, as Emily and Ethan joined her family for dinner, tensions hung in the air like a heavy fog. John, Emily's father, observed Ethan closely, his protective instincts still on high alert.

However, as the evening unfolded, Emily's family began to see the kindness, sincerity, and strength of character in Ethan. He shared stories of his pack, the challenges they faced, and his unwavering commitment to protecting them and Emily.

By the end of the evening, Emily's family had softened their stance, realizing that love could indeed transcend boundaries. While they were not entirely free of worry, they recognized that their daughter's happiness was deeply intertwined with Ethan's presence in her life.

As the moon continued to rise and fall, the unity between Ethan's pack and Emily's family strengthened. The two worlds that had once seemed irreconcilable were slowly finding common ground, all because of the love shared between Emily and Ethan.

With their loved ones standing by their side, Emily and Ethan were ready to face the impending showdown with Victor's pack. They knew that their love was their greatest strength, and they were determined to prove that it could overcome the boundaries of prejudice and fear.

Chapter 9: Secrets Unveiled

As the moon ascended into the night sky, casting its ethereal light over the forest, Emily and Ethan found themselves on the precipice of a fateful showdown with Victor's rival werewolf pack. Their unity with Ethan's pack and Emily's family had grown stronger, but secrets and revelations still lay hidden, waiting to be unveiled.

Emily couldn't shake the feeling that there was more to her own family's history than she had been told. Her father, John, had always been reticent about their lineage, especially when it came to their connection to the supernatural world of werewolves.

One evening, as they sat in the cozy living room of their cabin, Emily decided to broach the subject. "Dad," she began tentatively, "I've been thinking about our family's past. There's something you're not telling me, isn't there?"

John's expression shifted, a mix of hesitation and reluctance crossing his face. "Emily, there are things about our family that I've kept hidden to protect you."

Emily's curiosity was piqued. "Protect me from what, Dad? What is it that you're not telling me?"

John sighed deeply, realizing that it was time to reveal the family's hidden truths. "Our family has a long history with werewolves, Emily. Generations ago, one of our ancestors had a forbidden love affair with a werewolf, much like your relationship with Ethan."

Emily's eyes widened in astonishment. "You mean... I'm not the first in our family to fall in love with a werewolf?"

John nodded solemnly. "That's right. It's a part of our family's legacy that I tried to shield you from, fearing the consequences of such a connection. But perhaps it's time to embrace our history and acknowledge that love knows no boundaries."

Emily's heart swelled with a mix of emotions. She felt a profound connection to her ancestor and a sense of validation for her love for Ethan. Her father's revelation brought a newfound sense of understanding and acceptance, allowing her to face the impending showdown with Victor's pack with renewed determination.

In the werewolf community, Ethan had been grappling with his secrets. He had discovered an ancient prophecy that hinted at a powerful union between a werewolf and a human—a union that had the potential to bring about a new era of harmony and understanding between their worlds.

With this knowledge, Ethan realized that his love for Emily was not just a chance encounter but a part of a larger destiny. He confided in Clara, the pack's elder, about the prophecy and his belief in the strength of their love to fulfill it.

Clara regarded him with wise eyes. "Ethan, love has a way of transcending boundaries and changing the course of history. Perhaps you and Emily are the key to a future where werewolves and humans can coexist peacefully."

The weight of the prophecy hung heavy on Ethan's shoulders, but he felt a renewed sense of purpose. He knew that their love had the power to change their world, but first, they had to face Victor and his pack.

As the moon reached its zenith, Emily and Ethan shared their newfound secrets, strengthening the bond that connected them. With their families and pack members by their side, they were ready to confront the destiny that awaited them—an extraordinary love that could change their worlds forever.

Chapter 10: A Love Tested

The night of reckoning had arrived. Under the brilliant glow of the full moon, Emily, Ethan, and their united forces—Ethan's pack and Emily's family—stood at the edge of the forest, ready to confront Victor's rival werewolf pack. The air was thick with tension and anticipation as they ventured deeper into the heart of the woods.

Emily clung to Ethan's hand, her heart filled with a mix of fear and determination. Her family's acceptance of her love for him, coupled with the revelation of their family's history with werewolves, had given her the strength to face the impending battle.

Ethan, too, felt the weight of destiny on his shoulders. The ancient prophecy he had discovered spoke of a union between a werewolf and a human that could change the course of history. He knew that their love was at the center of it all, and it was a love that was about to be tested like never before.

As they approached Victor's territory, the tension in the air grew palpable. The rival pack awaited them in the clearing, their eyes filled with hostility and aggression. Victor, a towering figure with a cruel glint in his eye, stepped forward to confront Ethan.

"So, you've brought your human lover with you," Victor sneered. "You've become weak, Ethan, letting your heart cloud your judgment."

Ethan's gaze remained steady, his voice unwavering. "Love is not weakness, Victor. It's a source of strength, and it's what has united us."

The confrontation that followed was intense and brutal. Claws clashed, teeth gnashed, and the forest echoed with the sounds of a fierce battle. Emily, though frightened, stood her ground beside Ethan, determined to protect the love they had fought so hard to preserve.

Throughout the battle, the power of their unity became evident. The bonds of family, love, and friendship were strong, and they slowly began to turn the tide in their favor. Emily's family fought alongside Ethan's pack, their determination unwavering.

But Victor was a formidable adversary, and the battle raged on. Just as it seemed that all hope was lost, Emily's courage shone through. She summoned the strength within her and delivered a powerful speech about the power of love to unite and heal.

"Love knows no boundaries," Emily cried out, her voice ringing through the night. "It is the force that brings us together, that defies the divisions in our worlds. Our love can change our destinies, and it can end this senseless violence."

Her words resonated with the rival pack members, many of whom began to question Victor's ruthless leadership. The power of her speech combined with the unity of their forces began to erode Victor's hold over his pack.

In a final, climactic battle, Victor was defeated, not by physical force alone, but by the collective will of those who longed for a future where love could transcend their worlds.

As the moon began to wane, the rival pack members who had once followed Victor began to seek reconciliation. They recognized the truth in Emily's words and the strength of unity that had emerged from the chaos of battle.

In the end, Emily and Ethan's love prevailed, not just over their adversaries but over the prejudices and divisions that had threatened to tear their worlds apart. Their love had been tested and had emerged stronger than ever, paving the way for a future where werewolves and humans could coexist in harmony.

Under the fading moonlight, Emily and Ethan embraced their love a beacon of hope in a world where boundaries and secrets had been unveiled, and where the power of love had proven itself to be a force greater than any other.

Chapter 11: The Power of Unity

With the battle against Victor and his rival werewolf pack finally behind them, a sense of peace settled over the forest. The moon hung low in the night sky, its gentle light casting a serene glow over Emily, Ethan, and their united forces. The bonds of love, friendship, and family had proven stronger than any division, and unity had triumphed.

Victor, defeated and humbled, had been exiled from the territory, leaving his pack to seek a new path of cooperation and acceptance. The rival pack members who had once been adversaries were now allies, thanks to the power of Emily's words and the collective will to forge a better future.

Ethan's pack and Emily's family had discovered that love could transcend boundaries and that acceptance and understanding were possible even in the face of long-standing prejudices. The secrets of the past had been unveiled, and the legacy of love between werewolves and humans had been acknowledged.

Amid the newfound unity, Ethan and Emily's love shone brighter than ever. They knew that their relationship was not just a symbol of change but a testament to the power of love to overcome the most formidable challenges.

One evening, as Emily and Ethan stood beneath the moonlit sky, they shared a moment of reflection. "We did it, Ethan," Emily said with a smile. "We proved that love can change the world."

Ethan's eyes were filled with pride and adoration as he gazed at the woman he loved. "Yes, Emily, we did. Our love has brought about a new era of understanding between our worlds."

As the days turned into weeks and the weeks into months, the forest continued to thrive, its beauty a reflection of the harmony that had been achieved. Emily's family and Ethan's pack lived side by side, working together to protect their territory and maintain the balance between their worlds.

Emily had become a bridge between the human and werewolf communities, using her experiences to foster understanding and cooperation. Her determination to embrace her family's history and her love for Ethan not only changed her own life but also paved the way for a brighter future for all.

Under the moonlight, Emily and Ethan's love continued to flourish. They knew that their journey had been a test of love's endurance and that it had revealed the power of unity in the face of division. Their love had transcended boundaries and had proven that, together, they could change the world.

As they stood hand in hand, bathed in the gentle light of the moon, Emily and Ethan knew that their love story would be remembered as a testament to the enduring strength of love, the courage to confront prejudice, and the power of unity to bring about positive change in a world where the boundaries between human and supernatural were no longer insurmountable.

Chapter 12: A Future Together

With the power of love and unity, Emily and Ethan's worlds had transformed. The harmony between their families and packs had created a future filled with hope and possibilities. Under the moon's gentle gaze, they began to envision the life they could build together.

Ethan and Emily stood at the edge of the forest, a place that had once been a symbol of secrecy and separation but was now a testament to their enduring love. The moon hung low in the sky, casting its radiant light upon them.

"Ethan," Emily began, her voice filled with hope, "we've come so far together. Our love has overcome obstacles that once seemed insurmountable."

Ethan smiled, his eyes reflecting the same optimism. "Yes, Emily. We've shown that love and unity can bridge the divide between our worlds."

Emily's family and Ethan's pack had become one, embracing the values of cooperation, acceptance, and understanding. The once-secret love story between a human and a werewolf paved the way for a brighter future.

As they looked to the horizon, Emily and Ethan saw a world where humans and werewolves coexisted in harmony. The forest, once a place of secrets and shadows, was now a symbol of unity and shared purpose.

"We can build a life together, Ethan," Emily said, her heart full of joy. "A life where love knows no boundaries, and where our love story can inspire others to embrace acceptance and change."

Ethan nodded, his love for Emily shining brightly. "I want nothing more than to spend my life with you, Emily. To face every challenge and celebrate every triumph together."

Their lips met in a tender kiss, sealing their commitment to a future filled with love, unity, and shared dreams. As they held each other beneath the moonlight, Emily and Ethan knew that their love story had not only brought them together but had also transformed their worlds.

The moon, a silent witness to their journey, continued to rise and fall, casting its timeless light upon the forest they now called home. Emily and Ethan's love, ensnared by the night, had illuminated a path toward a future where love conquered all, and they were determined to walk it hand in hand.

Chapter 13: A Surprise Visit

As Emily and Ethan's love story continued to flourish, their lives were filled with moments of joy and tranquility in the moonlit forest. But one evening, as they were sharing a quiet moment by the serene pond where they had spent so many nights together, an unexpected visitor arrived.

A rustle in the bushes drew their attention, and they turned to see a figure emerging from the shadows. It was Clara, the elder of Ethan's pack, her wise eyes filled with a sense of purpose.

"Clara," Ethan greeted her warmly, "what brings you here tonight?"

Clara approached them, her demeanor both serious and gentle. "I have come with news, my dear," she said. "News that concerns both of you."

Emily and Ethan exchanged curious glances, their hearts filled with a mixture of anticipation and uncertainty.

"Long ago," Clara began, "there was a legend within our pack—a prophecy that spoke of a union between a werewolf and a human, a union that would bring about a new era of harmony between our worlds."

Ethan and Emily listened intently, their eyes locked on Clara.

"The prophecy also spoke of a sacred place," Clara continued, "a place where this union could be sealed and its power harnessed."

Emily's heart quickened as she realized the significance of Clara's words. "You mean... there's a place where we can make our love official, a place where we can fulfill the prophecy?"

Clara nodded, a knowing smile on her face. "Yes, my dear. It is known as the 'Sanctuary of the Moon,' a place hidden deep within the heart of the forest. There, under the full moon's light, your love can be sealed, and its power can be unleashed."

Ethan and Emily exchanged a look of awe and excitement. The idea of sealing their love in a place of such significance filled them with a sense of purpose and destiny.

"When can we go to this Sanctuary of the Moon?" Ethan asked eagerly.

Clara's eyes twinkled with anticipation. "The time is near. I will guide you both when the moon is at its fullest, and the Sanctuary's power is at its peak."

The prospect of fulfilling the prophecy
and sealing their love in the sacred place filled Emily and Ethan with a sense of exhilaration. Their love, once ensnared by the night, was now poised to shine as a beacon of hope and change for their worlds.

As they watched Clara disappear into the moonlit forest, Emily and Ethan knew that their journey was far from over. The Sanctuary of the Moon awaited them, and with it, the opportunity to make their love official and to embrace their destiny as a couple who could change the course of history.

Under the watchful eye of the moon, their love story continued to unfold, filled with surprises and the promise of a future where love would always prevail.

Chapter 14: Healing Wounds

In the weeks that followed Clara's revelation about the Sanctuary of the Moon, Emily, and Ethan eagerly anticipated the moment when they could fulfill the prophecy and make their love official. The promise of the sacred place had filled them with hope, but it also carried the weight of destiny.

During this time, Emily's family and Ethan's pack continued to work together, forging stronger bonds of friendship and cooperation. The wounds of the past were slowly healing, and the forest that had once been a symbol of secrecy and division was now a place of unity and shared purpose.

As the day of their journey to the Sanctuary of the Moon approached, Emily and Ethan spent their nights exploring the forest, finding comfort in each other's arms, and sharing their dreams for the future. They had faced challenges and overcome obstacles, but their love had remained unshaken.

One evening, as they stood by the serene pond, the moonlight casting a soft glow on the water, Emily spoke softly, "Ethan, I can't believe how far we've come. Our love has brought so much change and healing to our worlds."

Ethan nodded, his heart overflowing with love for her. "It's because of you, Emily. You've shown us all the power of love to transform our lives and bring about unity."

Their love had become a symbol of hope, and it had touched the hearts of those around them. As they continued to prepare for their journey to the Sanctuary of the Moon, they found themselves surrounded by love and support from both their families and their pack members.

The day of their journey arrived, and under the full moon's radiant light, they set out for the hidden sanctuary. Clara, the elder of Ethan's pack, led the way, her wisdom guiding them through the forest.

As they reached the sacred place, a sense of awe and reverence washed over Emily and Ethan. The sanctuary was a secluded grove, bathed in the moon's brilliance. In the center stood an ancient stone altar, weathered by time but still standing strong.

Clara explained, "This is where the prophecy foretells that your love can be sealed, and its power harnessed. Here, under the full moon, you can make your commitment to each other and to the destiny that awaits."

Emily and Ethan stood before the stone altar, their hearts filled with love and determination. They exchanged vows and promises, sealing their commitment with a kiss that felt like a promise to the moon itself.

As they kissed, the moon's light seemed to intensify, enveloping them in a warm embrace. The sanctuary's power flowed through them, filling them with a sense of purpose and destiny.

Their love, once ensnared by the night, had now been sanctified by the moon's light. It was a love that had endured challenges and overcome prejudice, a love that had changed their worlds and had the potential to change even more.

Under the watchful eye of the moon, Emily and Ethan knew that their love story had taken a new turn. Their journey was far from over, but they were ready to face whatever challenges and adventures lay ahead, united in their love and bound by the power of the Sanctuary of the Moon.

Chapter 15: A Promise Made

With their love sealed in the Sanctuary of the Moon, Emily and Ethan's bond had become stronger than ever. The ancient prophecy had been fulfilled, and the power of their love radiated like a beacon of hope in their worlds. But their journey was not yet complete, and there was one more promise they needed to make.

Under the moon's gentle glow, Emily and Ethan stood hand in hand in the sanctuary, feeling its ancient magic infusing their souls. Clara, the elder of Ethan's pack, watched over them with a knowing smile.

"Emily, Ethan," Clara began, "you have fulfilled the prophecy, and your love has already brought about significant change. But there is one more promise you must make."

Emily and Ethan exchanged a curious glance, their hearts open to whatever lay ahead.

Clara continued, "The prophecy also speaks of a commitment to foster understanding and cooperation between your worlds. It is a promise to work together to ensure that the harmony you've found here can spread beyond these woods."

Ethan nodded in agreement, his eyes locked with Emily's. "We promise," he said solemnly, "to continue building bridges of understanding between humans and werewolves, to foster acceptance, and to work toward a future where our love is not the exception but the norm."

Emily's voice echoed with the same determination. "We promise to be advocates for unity and change, to use our love story as a beacon of hope, and to inspire others to embrace acceptance and cooperation."

Clara smiled, her approval evident in her wise eyes. "With this promise, your love story is not only a testament to your love but also a symbol of a brighter future for your worlds. I do not doubt that you will continue to shine as beacons of hope and change."

As the moon reached its zenith, Emily and Ethan sealed their promise with a kiss, a vow to work tirelessly for the unity of their worlds. The sanctuary's magic seemed to swirl around them, infusing them with a renewed sense of purpose.

Their love story had already brought about profound change, but their commitment to their promise ensured that their journey was far from over. United by love and bound by destiny, Emily and Ethan were ready to face the adventures and challenges that lay ahead.

Under the moon's watchful gaze, they stepped out of the sanctuary, hand in hand, their hearts filled with determination and a promise to make a difference. Their love, once ensnared by the night, was now a guiding light, illuminating a path toward a future where acceptance and unity prevailed.

Chapter 16: A Magical Night

With their promise to foster understanding and cooperation between their worlds made in the sacred Sanctuary of the Moon, Emily and Ethan embarked on a new phase of their journey together. The moon continued to shine brightly in the night sky, guiding their way.

As they ventured deeper into the forest, their love seemed to take on a magical quality. The bonds of unity and acceptance they had forged between their families and packs had created an atmosphere of harmony in their lives.

One enchanting evening, as Emily and Ethan strolled hand in hand through the moonlit forest, they stumbled upon a clearing they had never seen before. The clearing was aglow with the soft light of fireflies, their tiny bodies twinkling like stars.

Emily gasped in wonder. "Ethan, it's like something out of a fairy tale."

Ethan smiled, his love for Emily shining in his eyes. "It's a magical night, just like our love."

As they stood amid the firefly-lit clearing, Emily felt a sense of wonder wash over her. She twirled around, laughing, as the fireflies danced around her like radiant fairies.

Ethan joined her, his laughter filling the night air. They danced together, their love for each other and the world around them making every moment feel like a dream.

The fireflies seemed to be drawn to them, forming a radiant halo of light that enveloped Emily and Ethan. It was as though the forest itself was celebrating their love, blessing them with a magical night to remember.

Under the canopy of stars and fireflies, Emily and Ethan shared a kiss that felt like a promise to the universe. It was a moment of pure magic, a testament to the power of love to transform the ordinary into the extraordinary.

As they held each other in the moonlit clearing, Emily and Ethan knew that their love story was far from ordinary. It was a love story that had defied boundaries, changed their worlds, and now, on this magical night, had shown them that the universe itself celebrated their love.

With their hearts filled with gratitude and wonder, they continued to dance and twirl beneath the moon and firefly-lit sky. Their love, once ensnared by the night, had now become a source of enchantment, a love that could make even the ordinary moments in life feel like pure magic.

Chapter 17: The Final Showdown

As Emily and Ethan's love continued to shine like a beacon of hope and change in their worlds, a storm began to brew on the horizon. News had reached them that a new threat was emerging, one that threatened to undo the unity they had worked so hard to achieve.

A rogue group of werewolves, led by a powerful and vengeful alpha, had gathered in the depths of the forest. This alpha, known as Fenrir, held a deep grudge against both humans and Ethan's pack for their role in Victor's exile.

Word of Fenrir's intentions had reached Ethan's pack, and they knew that a confrontation was inevitable. Emily's family, having come to accept their connection to the supernatural world, also stood ready to defend their newfound unity.

One night, as the moon hung low in the sky, Emily and Ethan met with Clara, the elder of Ethan's pack, to discuss the looming threat. Clara's eyes were filled with concern as she spoke of Fenrir's desire for revenge.

"Fenrir is powerful and ruthless," Clara warned. "He seeks to tear down the bridges of understanding we have built and plunge us back into a world of division and conflict."

Ethan's jaw tightened with determination. "We cannot let that happen, Clara. We've come too far to allow one alpha's hatred to undo everything we've worked for."

Emily, too, was resolute. "Our love is a symbol of change and unity. We will stand together to protect it and ensure that Fenrir's plan fails."

With Clara's guidance, Ethan's pack and Emily's family began preparations for the impending showdown. The forest, once a place of secrets and division, was now a fortress of unity and determination.

As the days passed, the tension in the forest grew, and the showdown with Fenrir and his rogue pack drew nearer. Emily and Ethan knew that this battle would be their greatest test yet, but they were ready to face it together, with their love as their guiding light.

Under the moon's watchful eye, Emily and Ethan, along with their united forces, steeled themselves for the final confrontation with Fenrir. They were determined to protect the harmony they had fought so hard to achieve and to prove that love and unity could prevail even in the face of the most formidable challenges.

The night of reckoning was fast approaching, and the forest, once again, held its breath in anticipation of the showdown between love and hatred, unity and division. Emily and Ethan knew that their love story had become a symbol of hope, and they were willing to fight with all their strength to ensure that it endured.

Chapter 18: A New Beginning

As the night of the showdown with Fenrir's rogue pack drew near, the moon hung heavy in the sky, casting an eerie glow over the forest. Emily and Ethan, their love unwavering, stood at the forefront of their united forces, ready to defend the unity they had fought so hard to achieve.

The tension in the air was palpable as Fenrir's pack approached, their eyes filled with hostility and rage. Fenrir himself, a formidable figure with eyes as cold as ice, stepped forward to confront Ethan.

"Ethan," Fenrir growled, "you've become weak, allying with humans and defying the laws of our kind. I will put an end to this madness and reclaim what is rightfully mine."

Ethan's voice rang with unwavering resolve. "Fenrir, you're blinded by hatred. Love and unity are not weaknesses; they are our greatest strengths. I won't let you destroy the harmony we've built."

The battle that followed was fierce. Claws clashed, teeth gnashed, and the forest echoed with the sounds of combat. Emily, her heart pounding with fear and determination, fought beside Ethan, their love giving them the strength to face the overwhelming odds.

As the battle raged on, Emily's family and Ethan's pack demonstrated their unity, fighting with an unwavering commitment to protect the love that had brought them together. The forest, once a place of secrets and division, now bore witness to a battle of epic proportions, where love and unity clashed with hatred and vengeance.

Amid the chaos, Clara, the elder of Ethan's pack, confronted Fenrir, her eyes filled with a mix of sorrow and determination. "Fenrir," she implored, "you don't have to go down this path. Love and acceptance can heal the wounds of the past."

Fenrir, however, remained steadfast in his anger. "It's too late for me, Clara. I've made my choice."

But Clara's words had planted a seed of doubt in Fenrir's heart, and as the battle raged on, he began to question the path he had chosen. The unity and love he witnessed among the humans and werewolves made him wonder if there was another way.

As the moon reached its zenith, Emily and Ethan's love, along with the unwavering unity of their forces, began to turn the tide of battle. The rogue werewolves, disheartened by Fenrir's wavering resolve, began to question their allegiance.

In a final, climactic confrontation, Fenrir, torn between hatred and doubt, was defeated not by force but by the power of love and unity. With the rogue pack's defeat, the forest was once again bathed in the moon's serene light, a symbol of hope and harmony.

Fenrir, his anger replaced by remorse, accepted exile, leaving the forest in search of a path of redemption and self-discovery. Emily and Ethan's love, and the unity they had inspired, had shown him that change was possible, even for those consumed by hatred.

With the battle won and the unity of their worlds preserved, Emily and Ethan stood together in the moonlit forest, their love stronger than ever. Their journey had been filled with challenges and trials, but it had also been a testament to the enduring power of love to overcome even the darkest of obstacles.

As the moonlight bathed them in its gentle glow, Emily and Ethan knew that they were at the dawn of a new beginning. Their love story had brought about profound change, and their promise to foster understanding and cooperation between their worlds had been fulfilled.

Under the watchful eye of the moon, Emily and Ethan looked toward a future where love and unity would always prevail, a future where their love story was not just a symbol of change but a living testament to the extraordinary power of love to transform hearts and worlds.

Their love, once ensnared by the night, had now become a guiding light, illuminating a path toward a brighter and more harmonious future for all.

Chapter 19: A Proposal

With the battle against Fenrir and his rogue pack behind them, Emily and Ethan's love had proven unbreakable. The moon, which had witnessed every twist and turn of their journey, now shone brightly in the night sky, illuminating the path to their future together.

In the days that followed, the forest basked in a newfound sense of peace and unity. Emily's family and Ethan's pack continued to work together, forging bonds of friendship and cooperation that grew stronger with each passing day.

Emily and Ethan knew that their love had been tested and had emerged stronger than ever. Their promise to foster understanding and acceptance between humans and werewolves had become a reality, and their love story served as a source of inspiration for all who knew them.

One evening, as they strolled hand in hand through the moonlit forest, Ethan stopped in a small, secluded glade bathed in the moon's gentle light. He turned to Emily, his eyes filled with love and determination.

"Emily," he began, his voice trembling with emotion, "our journey together has been filled with challenges and triumphs, but through it all, our love has remained unwavering."

Emily gazed into Ethan's eyes, her heart swelling with love for him. "Yes, Ethan, our love has endured, and it has brought about so much change and hope."

Ethan knelt before Emily, his heart laid bare. "Emily, I want to spend the rest of my life with you. Will you do me the honor of becoming my mate, not just in heart but in every sense of the word?"

Emily's eyes filled with tears of joy as she realized the significance of Ethan's words. "Yes, Ethan," she replied with unwavering certainty, "I want to be with you always, to share in every aspect of your world and your love."

Ethan's face lit up with happiness as he produced a small, intricately carved wooden box. With trembling hands, he opened it to reveal a delicate silver ring adorned with a moonstone, its ethereal glow reflecting the moonlight.

"Emily," Ethan said, his voice filled with love, "this ring represents the bond between us, a bond that transcends boundaries and unites our hearts. Will you marry me?"

Tears of joy streamed down Emily's cheeks as she held out her hand, allowing Ethan to place the ring on her finger. It fits perfectly as if it had been crafted for her alone.

"Yes, Ethan," she whispered, her heart overflowing with love, "I will marry you."

With the moon as their witness, Emily and Ethan sealed their promise with a passionate kiss. The forest, which had seen their love story unfold, seemed to embrace them in a warm, congratulatory glow.

Their love, once ensnared by the night, had now taken a new turn. They were ready to face the future together, as mates, as champions of love and unity, and as a symbol of the enduring power of love to transcend boundaries and change the world.

Under the moon's radiant light, Emily and Ethan embraced their future with open hearts, their love story continuing to inspire and uplift all who crossed their path.

Chapter 20: Wedding Preparations

With Emily and Ethan's engagement celebrated under the moon's radiant light, the forest echoed with the promise of their future together. The news of their upcoming wedding filled the hearts of their loved ones with joy, and preparations for the grand celebration began in earnest.

Emily's family and Ethan's pack worked side by side to plan a wedding that would be a symbol of unity and love, a testament to the harmony they had achieved. The forest, once a place of secrets and division, was now filled with excitement and anticipation.

The date for the wedding was set to coincide with a full moon, a nod to the role the moon had played in their love story. The ceremony would take place in the same glade where Ethan had proposed, bathed in the moon's gentle light.

Emily, with the help of her family and newfound friends among the werewolves, chose a gown that shimmered like moonlight itself. It was a dress that reflected the unity of their worlds, with delicate lace and silver embroidery.

Ethan, along with his pack, prepared for the wedding with a sense of pride and anticipation. They ensured that every detail, from the decorations to the feast, would be a reflection of the love and unity that had brought them all together.

As the days passed, Emily and Ethan's love story continued to inspire those around them. The forest, once a place of division, had become a sanctuary of unity, and their wedding was a symbol of the love that could
conquer even the greatest challenges.

One evening, as Emily and Ethan stood by the serene pond, they reflected on their journey together. Emily spoke softly, her voice filled with love and gratitude, "Ethan, our love has brought so much change and healing to our worlds. I can't wait to begin this new chapter as your mate."

Ethan smiled, his eyes filled with adoration. "Emily, you are the light of my life. Our love has shown us that anything is possible, and I can't wait to spend eternity with you."

Under the moon's watchful gaze, they shared a tender kiss, sealing their love and commitment to each other. Their wedding day was fast approaching, and their hearts were filled with excitement and anticipation.

As the moon continued to rise and fall, Emily and Ethan's love story became a beacon of hope and change, a testament to the enduring power of love to transform hearts and worlds. Their wedding day would not only mark the beginning of their life together as mates but also a celebration of the unity and love that had brought their worlds together.

Under the moon's radiant light, they knew that their love story was far from over. It was a story of love, unity, and the promise of a future where acceptance and cooperation would always prevail, a future where their love would continue to shine as a guiding light for all.

Chapter 21: Tensions Rise

As the day of Emily and Ethan's wedding approached, a sense of anticipation filled the moonlit forest. The preparations were in full swing, and the glade where the ceremony would take place was adorned with flowers, lanterns, and an air of unity and love.

However, not all was well in their harmonious world. Rumors had begun to circulate about a faction of werewolves who were opposed to the union between a human and a werewolf. This faction, led by a charismatic but dangerous alpha named Lucius, believed that such a union was a threat to the traditional way of life among werewolves.

Tensions simmered beneath the surface as the wedding day neared. Emily and Ethan were aware of the growing unease but remained determined to celebrate their love and unity. They believed that their wedding could serve as a powerful message of acceptance and change.

One evening, as they walked through the moonlit forest, Emily expressed her concerns to Ethan. "Ethan, I can't ignore the tension that's been building. What if Lucius and his faction try to disrupt our wedding?"

Ethan tightened his grip on Emily's hand, his expression determined. "We won't let anyone ruin our special day, Emily. Our love is stronger than any opposition, and we have the support of our families and pack members."

The forest, which had witnessed their entire love story, seemed to hold its breath in anticipation of what lay ahead. The moon, a silent observer of their journey, continued to rise and fall, casting its serene light over the world.

As the wedding day drew closer, the tension in the forest grew. Emily and Ethan's families and pack members remained vigilant, ready to protect the unity they had worked so hard to achieve.

But Lucius and his faction were not to be underestimated. They were determined to stop the wedding, viewing it as a threat to their way of life. The atmosphere in the forest became charged with uncertainty, and the glade where the ceremony would take place seemed to hold its breath.

Under the moon's watchful gaze, Emily and Ethan faced a new challenge, one that tested the strength of their love and the unity they had fought so hard to achieve. The wedding day, once a symbol of hope and change, now held the potential for conflict and upheaval.

As they stood together, their love stronger than ever, Emily and Ethan were prepared to face whatever challenges lay ahead. They knew that their love story had become a symbol of unity and acceptance, and they were determined to ensure that their wedding day would be a testament to the enduring power of love to conquer even the greatest of obstacles.

Chapter 22: The Big Day

The day of Emily and Ethan's wedding had finally arrived, and the moon shone brightly in the sky, casting its serene light over the moonlit forest. The glade where the ceremony would take place was adorned with flowers, lanterns, and the hopes and dreams of those who believed in the power of love and unity.

Despite the tensions that had been brewing, Emily and Ethan were determined to celebrate their love and send a message of acceptance to all who opposed it. They believed that their wedding could be a turning point, a moment when their love and unity would prevail.

As Emily prepared for her family's cabin, her heart filled with a mixture of excitement and nervousness. She wore a gown that shimmered like moonlight itself, a symbol of the love that had brought her and Ethan together.

Meanwhile, Ethan and his pack members stood at the glade, ready to protect the unity they had worked so hard to achieve. The tension in the forest was palpable, but their determination to see the wedding through remained unshaken.

As the sun began to set and the moon rose higher in the sky, guests from both Emily's family and Ethan's pack gathered in the glade. The atmosphere was charged with a sense of anticipation, and the moon seemed to cast its blessing over the gathering.

Emily, escorted by her father, made her way to the glade. Her heart swelled with emotion as she saw Ethan waiting for her, his eyes filled with love and adoration. The forest, which had witnessed every twist and turn of their love story, seemed to hold its breath in anticipation.

The ceremony began with a heartfelt exchange of vows, where Emily and Ethan promised to stand together, united in love and acceptance. Their words resonated with those gathered, serving as a reminder of the power of love to transcend boundaries.

But just as the ceremony reached its most poignant moment, when Emily and Ethan were about to exchange rings, a rustle in the trees at the edge of the glade drew everyone's attention. Lucius, the alpha of the opposing faction, and his followers emerged from the shadows.

"Stop this madness!" Lucius roared, his eyes filled with anger. "This union is a threat to our way of life, and we won't allow it to happen!"

Tensions reached a breaking point as Emily and Ethan's loved ones and pack members faced off with Lucius and his faction. The moon, a silent witness to the unfolding drama, continued to shine down upon them.

During the confrontation, Emily and Ethan stood together, their love unwavering. They knew that this moment was a test of their love and the unity they had fought so hard to achieve.

Under the moon's watchful gaze, Emily and Ethan's wedding day had taken an unexpected turn, one that would determine the fate of their love and the message they sought to send to their worlds. The forest, which had been a place of division and unity, now held its breath, waiting to see if love would conquer all.

Chapter 23: Honeymoon Bliss

Despite the tense interruption during their wedding ceremony, Emily and Ethan's love had proven stronger than any opposition. The moon, which had watched over their love story, seemed to bless their union as the conflict at the glade was resolved peacefully.

Lucius and his followers, moved by the love and unity displayed by Emily and Ethan's families and pack members, had a change of heart. They realized that their fears had been unfounded and that love and acceptance could coexist with tradition.

Lucius, in a surprising turn of events, offered his blessings to Emily and Ethan, recognizing that their love was a powerful force for change. With his support, the wedding ceremony continued, and Emily and Ethan exchanged their rings and vows under the moon's serene light.

As the newlyweds, Emily and Ethan embarked on their honeymoon, a journey that would take them to new and exciting places. They chose to explore the world together, believing that their love story could continue to inspire and bring about positive change beyond the moonlit forest.

Their first destination was a picturesque coastal town, where they rented a cozy cottage by the sea. The moonlit nights were enchanting, and the sound of the waves crashing against the shore provided a soothing backdrop to their romantic evenings.

During the day, they explored the quaint town, strolling hand in hand through cobblestone streets, and enjoying the local cuisine. They sampled freshly caught seafood and indulged in sweet pastries from a charming bakery.

One evening, as they stood on the beach, the moon reflecting off the water, Emily turned to Ethan with a smile. "Ethan, our journey together has been filled with challenges, but it has also been a testament to the power of love and unity."

Ethan wrapped his arm around her waist, pulling her close. "Yes, Emily, our love story has shown us that love can conquer even the greatest obstacles. We've inspired change not only in our worlds but also in ourselves."

Their honeymoon was a time of bliss and reflection, a moment to celebrate the love that had brought them together and the unity that had transformed their lives. They knew that their journey was far from over and that they would continue to face challenges, but they were ready to face them together.

Under the moon's gentle light, Emily and Ethan's love story had entered a new chapter, one filled with the promise of adventure, unity, and the enduring power of love to change hearts and worlds. They were ready to embrace whatever the future held, knowing that their love would always prevail.

Chapter 24: A New Life

As Emily and Ethan returned from their honeymoon, they were greeted by a warm and welcoming homecoming in the moonlit forest. The tensions that had once threatened their love and unity had dissipated, and their love
story had become a source of inspiration and hope for their worlds.

Emily's family and Ethan's pack had continued to build on the unity they had forged, working together to ensure a future where love and acceptance prevailed. The forest, which had been a place of secrets and division, was now a symbol of unity and cooperation.

Emily and Ethan settled into their life as mates, combining their worlds and traditions. Emily learned about the ways of the werewolves, while Ethan embraced human customs and culture. Their love was a bridge between their worlds, a testament to the power of love to transcend boundaries.

Emily continued her work as a botanist, studying the unique flora of the moonlit forest and sharing her discoveries with the scientific community. Her research had become a symbol of the harmony between humans and werewolves, a testament to what could be achieved when love and acceptance were embraced.

Ethan, in his role as a leader of the werewolf pack, continued to advocate for unity and understanding between humans and werewolves. He worked tirelessly to ensure that the harmony they had achieved was maintained and that prejudice and fear were replaced with acceptance and cooperation.

One evening, as Emily and Ethan stood by the serene pond where their love story had begun, they reflected on their journey together. Emily spoke softly, her voice filled with love and gratitude, "Ethan, our love has brought so much change and healing to our worlds. I couldn't have asked for a better mate."

Ethan smiled, his eyes filled with adoration. "Emily, you are my everything. Our love has shown us that love knows no boundaries and that acceptance and unity are possible."

As they watched the moon rise in the sky, they knew that their love story was far from over. It was a story of love, unity, and the promise of a future where acceptance and cooperation would always prevail.

Under the moon's watchful gaze, Emily and Ethan embraced their new life together, knowing that their love would continue to shine as a guiding light for all who crossed their path. Their love, once ensnared by the night, had now become a beacon of hope, illuminating a path toward a brighter and more harmonious future for all.

Chapter 25: An Unexpected Twist

Emily and Ethan's life together in the moonlit forest was filled with joy and purpose. Their love story had become a symbol of unity and acceptance, and their worlds had continued to evolve in positive ways. However, just when they thought their journey was becoming peaceful, an unexpected twist threw their lives into uncertainty.

One moonlit night, as they enjoyed a quiet moment by the pond, a messenger from a neighboring supernatural community arrived with troubling news. A long-standing conflict between two powerful supernatural factions had escalated, threatening to spill over into their forest.

The messenger explained, "Emily, Ethan, your love story has inspired hope and change in our world as well. We seek your help in mediating a peaceful resolution to this conflict."

Emily and Ethan exchanged worried glances, their hearts heavy with the responsibility that had been thrust upon them. They knew that their love story had become a symbol of unity, but they had not anticipated being called upon to play a role in the affairs of other supernatural communities.

With a sense of duty, Emily and Ethan agreed to meet with the leaders of the opposing factions. They hoped that their love and unity could serve as a beacon of hope and inspire a peaceful resolution to the conflict.

As they ventured into the heart of the neighboring supernatural territory, Emily and Ethan faced challenges they had not encountered before. The factions were deeply entrenched in their beliefs and grievances, and the tension in the air was palpable.

Emily and Ethan knew that they needed to find common ground, to bridge the gap between the factions just as they had done in their worlds. Their love and unity had the power to inspire change, but they would need all their strength and determination to succeed.

Under the moon's watchful gaze, Emily and Ethan embarked on a new chapter of their journey, one that would test the limits of their love and the power of unity. They were ready to face this unexpected twist in their lives, knowing that their love had the potential to bring about positive change, not only in their worlds but in others as well.

Chapter 26: The Miracle of Life

As Emily and Ethan ventured deeper into the territory of the warring supernatural factions, they felt the weight of responsibility on their shoulders. They knew that their love story had inspired hope, but they were uncertain if it could bring about the peace that was desperately needed.

Upon their arrival, they were met with skepticism and suspicion from the leaders of the opposing factions. The leaders, Amara and Gabriel, had been locked in a bitter conflict for generations, and the scars of their feud ran deep.

Emily and Ethan presented their case, emphasizing the power of love and unity, and how their own love story had transcended boundaries. They implored Amara and Gabriel to find a way to coexist peacefully, for the sake of their supernatural community and the generations to come.

Amara, a formidable and proud leader, was initially resistant to the idea. "Love is not enough to heal the wounds of the past," she argued. "Our grievances run too deep."

But Gabriel, a wise and contemplative leader, saw something in Emily and Ethan's love story that resonated with him. He recalled a time when the factions had lived in harmony and unity.

"Amara, perhaps it is time for us to set aside our differences," Gabriel said, his voice filled with a newfound hope. "Emily and Ethan's love story reminds us of what we once were—a united and peaceful community. Maybe it's time to embrace change and heal the divisions that have torn us apart."

As the leaders contemplated their words, a miracle occurred. During their discussions, a young supernatural child, born of parents from opposing factions, was discovered in the forest nearby. The child's birth was a rare and powerful symbol—a symbol of love transcending boundaries.

Amara and Gabriel gazed upon the newborn with awe and wonder. The sight of the child, born of love between their factions, was a profound reminder that unity was not only possible but also necessary for the survival and happiness of their people.

With tears in her eyes, Amara spoke, her voice filled with emotion. "Perhaps it is time for us to put aside our grievances and embrace a new path—a path of unity, acceptance, and cooperation, just as this child's parents have."

Gabriel nodded in agreement, his heart touched by the miracle before them. "We owe it to this child and to future generations to create a world where love and acceptance prevail."

Under the moon's serene light, Emily and Ethan's love story had worked a miracle—a miracle of life that had the power to heal even the deepest of wounds. Amara and Gabriel, inspired by this miracle, agreed to work toward a peaceful resolution to their conflict.

As Emily and Ethan left the supernatural community, they knew that their journey was far from over. They had once again witnessed the transformative power of love and unity, and they were filled with hope for a future where acceptance and cooperation would always prevail.

Their love story, which had become a symbol of change and unity, had now played a role in bringing about a miracle of life, a testament to the enduring power of love to transcend boundaries and transform hearts and worlds.

Chapter 27: Facing the Future

With the successful resolution of the conflict between the warring supernatural factions, Emily and Ethan returned to their moonlit forest with a renewed sense of purpose. Their journey had taken unexpected turns, but their love had continued to inspire change and bring hope to their worlds.

The forest, once a place of secrets and division, had evolved into a sanctuary of unity and cooperation. The story of Emily and Ethan's love had become legendary, a symbol of the enduring power of love to transform hearts and worlds.

As they stood by the serene pond where their love story had begun, Emily and Ethan reflected on their experiences. Emily spoke softly, her voice filled with gratitude, "Ethan, our journey has been filled with challenges and miracles. I'm grateful for the love and unity that we've been able to inspire."

Ethan smiled, his eyes reflecting the moon's gentle light. "Emily, our love has shown us that anything is possible when hearts are open to change. Our future together is a testament to that."

The moon, a silent witness to their entire journey, continued to shine down upon them, casting its serene light over the world. Emily and Ethan knew that their love story was not just their own but a story of hope and transformation that could inspire others.

As they looked toward the future, Emily and Ethan were filled with a sense of purpose. They were ready to face whatever challenges lay ahead, knowing that their love would always guide them.

Under the moon's watchful gaze, they embraced the promise of a future where love, acceptance, and unity would always prevail. Their love story had become a beacon of hope, a testament to the extraordinary power of love to transcend boundaries and change the world.

With hearts full of love and determination, Emily and Ethan walked hand in hand into the moonlit forest, ready to face the future together, knowing that their love would continue to shine as a guiding light for all who crossed their path.

Chapter 28: A Love that Endures

Time passed in the moonlit forest, and Emily and Ethan's love story continued to inspire those around them. The unity they had fostered between their worlds remained steadfast, and their love had become an enduring symbol of acceptance and change.

Emily's family and Ethan's pack had become a closely-knit community, working together to ensure that the harmony they had achieved endured. The forest, once a place of secrets and division, was now a testament to the power of love and unity.

As the years went by, Emily and Ethan's love only deepened. They faced challenges and triumphs, joys and sorrows, but through it all, their bond remained unbreakable. Their love was a testament to the enduring power of love to transcend boundaries and transform lives.

One evening, as they stood by the serene pond where their love story had begun, Emily and Ethan reflected on their journey together. Emily spoke softly, her voice filled with love, "Ethan, our love has brought so much change and healing to our worlds. I'm grateful for every moment we've shared."

Ethan smiled, his eyes filled with adoration. "Emily, you are the love of my life. Our journey has shown us that love knows no boundaries, and our story will continue to inspire others."

Under the moon's gentle light, they shared a tender kiss, sealing their love and commitment to each other once more. Their love story was not just a tale of their romance but a story of hope, transformation, and a future where acceptance and cooperation would always prevail.

As they looked toward the horizon, Emily and Ethan knew that their love would continue to endure, a beacon of light in a world that sometimes needed a reminder of the power of love to conquer even the greatest challenges.

With hearts full of love and gratitude, they walked hand in hand into the moonlit forest, ready to face whatever the future held, knowing that their love would always shine as a guiding light for all who crossed their path. Their love, once ensnared by the night, had become a love that endured through all the seasons of life.

Chapter 29: A Legacy of Love

Emily and Ethan's love story had become a legend in the moonlit forest, a symbol of unity, acceptance, and the enduring power of love. Their journey had inspired change not only in their worlds but in the hearts of many who had heard their tale.

As the years passed, Emily and Ethan continued to lead their community with love and wisdom. Their families had grown, and their pack had expanded, each member cherishing the legacy of unity and acceptance that had been built.

One day, Emily and Ethan gathered their loved ones by the serene pond to reflect on their journey. Emily spoke with a heart full of gratitude, "Ethan, our love story has brought so much hope and transformation. I'm proud of the legacy we've created."

Ethan nodded, his eyes filled with love and pride. "Emily, our love has shown us that love knows no boundaries, and it has become a legacy that will endure for generations."

Their children and pack members, inspired by their story, had taken up the mantle of unity and acceptance, ensuring that the forest remained a place of harmony and cooperation.

The moon, a silent observer of their journey, continued to cast its serene light over the world, a reminder of the love that had transformed the moonlit forest.

As Emily and Ethan looked around at their loved ones, they knew that their love story had become a legacy—a legacy of love, unity, and the enduring power of love to bring about positive change.

Under the moon's watchful gaze, they embraced the promise of a future where love, acceptance, and cooperation would always prevail. Their love, once ensnared by the night, had become a legacy that would endure through the ages, a testament to the extraordinary power of love to transcend boundaries and change the world.

With hearts full of love and hope, they walked hand in hand into the moonlit forest, knowing that their legacy of love would continue to shine as a guiding light for all who crossed their path. Their love story had become a legacy, a story of love that would endure for all time.

Chapter 30: Forever and Always

As the years turned into decades and the moon continued its eternal journey across the night sky, Emily and Ethan's love remained as strong as ever. Their legacy of love, unity, and acceptance had become a cornerstone of their community, a guiding light in a world that sometimes needed a reminder of the power of love to heal and transform.

Their own family had grown, with children and grandchildren who cherished the story of Emily and Ethan's love. Each generation carried forward the values of acceptance and cooperation, ensuring that the moonlit forest remained a sanctuary of harmony.

One evening, under the silvery light of the moon, Emily and Ethan sat by the serene pond, hand in hand, reflecting on their journey together. Emily's eyes sparkled with a lifetime of memories as she spoke, "Ethan, our love has been a gift, a source of hope and change for our worlds. I'm grateful for every moment we've shared."

Ethan's voice was filled with love and wisdom as he replied, "Emily, you are the love of my life, and our journey has shown us that love knows no boundaries. Our story will continue to inspire generations to come."

Their love had weathered the tests of time, and they knew that their bond was eternal. The moon, which had watched over them throughout their love story, continued to cast its serene light over the world, a silent witness to the enduring power of love.

As they gazed at the moon and each other, Emily and Ethan were filled with a sense of peace and contentment. Their love story had become a part of the fabric of their community, a legacy of love that would endure forever.

Under the moon's watchful gaze, they embraced the promise of an eternal love, one that transcended the boundaries of time and space. Their love, once ensnared by the night, had become a love that would last forever and always.

With hearts full of love and gratitude, they leaned in for a tender kiss, sealing their love and commitment to each other once more. Their love story had become a testament to the extraordinary power of love to conquer all obstacles, a story that would be told for generations to come.

And as the moon continued its journey, casting its light over the moonlit forest, Emily and Ethan's love remained a timeless and enduring love that would shine as a guiding star for all who crossed their path. Forever and always.

Chapter 1: Love From The Other Side: An astral Projection Romance: The Unexplained Connection

In the quiet town of Willowbrook, nestled beneath the shadow of a forested hill, Sarah Mitchell lived a life that appeared quite ordinary. She was an artist, known for her vivid paintings of landscapes and dreamscapes. Her days were filled with brushes, canvases, and the soothing sounds of a nearby creek.

But there was a part of Sarah's life that was anything but ordinary. For as long as she could remember, she had experienced dreams that were vivid beyond explanation. In these dreams, she wandered through ethereal landscapes, bathed in the soft glow of an otherworldly moon.

It was in these dreams that she encountered him—Ethan, a man she had never met in the waking world. His presence was a constant, a familiar stranger who haunted her dreamscape like a guardian spirit. His eyes, a mesmerizing shade of green, held secrets she longed to uncover.

Night after night, Sarah found herself drawn into conversations with Ethan amidst the surreal beauty of her dream world. They spoke of art, of desires, and of the mysteries that lay beyond the realm of the ordinary. She felt a connection with him that defied reason, a connection that stirred her heart and intrigued her mind.

Sarah's friends often teased her about her vivid dreams, dismissing them as the result of an overactive imagination. But to Sarah, these dreams were more than mere fantasies; they were a window into a world she couldn't explain.

One evening, as she sat by her easel, attempting to capture the elusive colors of her dreams on canvas, her best friend, Emma, visited her. Emma was a practical woman, the yin to Sarah's artistic yang. She raised an eyebrow as she examined Sarah's latest painting, a surreal landscape bathed in the soft, ethereal light of her dreams.

"You've been obsessed with these dreams lately, Sarah," Emma remarked, her voice tinged with concern. "Maybe it's time to take a break from your nocturnal adventures and focus on the real world."

Sarah sighed, her eyes still fixed on the canvas. "I know, Emma, but there's something about these dreams, about Ethan. It's as if he's a part of me, and I can't simply turn away."

As the two friends conversed, Sarah couldn't help but feel that her connection with Ethan was more profound than anyone could understand. Little did she know that her life was about to take a turn into the unexplained, leading her on a journey she never could have anticipated.

Chapter 2: Dreams and Desires

Sarah's fascination with her dreams intensified with each passing night. She continued to visit the ethereal realm where she met Ethan, and their conversations grew more intimate, revealing their deepest desires and fears.

In the dream world, Sarah and Ethan walked through meadows adorned with luminescent flowers that glowed like stars. The sky above them was a canvas of colors that defied earthly description. It was in this surreal landscape that they bared their souls to each other.

One moonlit night, as they sat on a grassy hill overlooking a tranquil lake, Sarah couldn't contain her curiosity any longer. "Ethan," she began, her voice quivering with anticipation, "there's something about you, about us, that I can't quite grasp. It's as if we're connected on a level that defies explanation."

Ethan, his eyes filled with a mixture of longing and understanding, nodded. "I feel it too, Sarah. Our connection is beyond the boundaries of the waking world. It's a bond that transcends time and space."

As they gazed at the reflection of the moon in the lake's mirror-like surface, Sarah dared to ask the question that had been plaguing her thoughts. "Ethan, do you think we'll ever meet in the real world? Is there a place for us beyond these dreams?"

Ethan's expression grew somber, and he reached out to gently cup Sarah's cheek. "I wish I could give you a definitive answer, Sarah. But our connection, as beautiful as it is, exists in a realm between reality and the unknown. I fear that the boundaries that separate our worlds may be too rigid to cross."

Tears welled up in Sarah's eyes, and she leaned into Ethan's touch, savoring the warmth of his presence. "Even if we can never be together in the waking world, I cherish these moments with you, Ethan. You've awakened a part of my soul I never knew existed."

Ethan smiled tenderly, his fingers brushing away her tears. "And you, Sarah, have shown me the beauty of the human heart. Our connection may remain a mystery, but our love is real, and it's a force that defies explanation."

As the moon continued its silent journey across the night sky, Sarah and Ethan shared a passionate kiss, sealing their connection in the dream world. Little did they know that their journey was far from over and that their love would lead them to uncover the secrets of a realm beyond their wildest dreams.

Chapter 3: The Secret World of Astral Projection

Sarah's fascination with the enigmatic Ethan and her inexplicable dreams led her to delve deeper into the mysteries that surrounded her nightly encounters. She was determined to understand the nature of their connection and the ethereal realm they shared.

In search of answers, Sarah turned to the internet and began researching the phenomenon of astral projection. Late nights were spent poring over articles, books, and forums dedicated to this mystical practice. She discovered that astral projection was the ability to separate one's consciousness from their physical body and explore the astral plane—an otherworldly dimension that existed beyond the confines of the physical world.

Driven by curiosity, Sarah sought guidance from a local spiritual guide, an elderly woman named Madame Serena, who was rumored to know the astral realm. Sarah described her dreams and the connection she felt with Ethan, hoping that Madame Serena could provide insights.

Madame Serena, with her eyes clouded in a milky haze, listened intently to Sarah's story. She nodded slowly as if recognizing a hidden truth. "Child," she began in a voice that seemed to echo from a distant place, "what you're experiencing is indeed astral projection—a journey of the soul beyond the limits of the physical world."

Sarah leaned closer, eager to learn more. "But, Madame Serena, what does it mean? And who is Ethan? Is he real?"

The spiritual guide smiled knowingly. "The astral realm is a place where the boundaries of reality blur, and connections that defy explanation are forged. Ethan may be a soul you've encountered on your astral journeys—a kindred spirit from another plane of existence."

Sarah's heart raced with excitement and apprehension. Could it be that her dreams were glimpses into a hidden world—one where her connection with Ethan was real? She yearned to explore this realm further, to bridge the gap between her dreams and reality.

Madame Serena offered to teach Sarah the art of controlled astral projection, guiding her on a journey to the ethereal realm. Sarah, filled with a sense of purpose, embraced the opportunity, determined to uncover the truth of her connection with Ethan and the secrets that lay beyond the veil of the astral plane.

As Sarah delved deeper into the world of astral projection, she would soon discover that the boundaries between dreams and reality were more fluid than she had ever imagined. Her journey had only just begun, and she was on the brink of unlocking a world of wonder and mysteries that defied the laws of the physical realm.

Chapter 4: A Love Beyond Reality

Sarah's training in astral projection under Madame Serena's guidance was a revelation. With each session, she learned to separate her consciousness from her physical body and enter the ethereal realm with greater ease. Her dreams became a portal to a world where her connection with Ethan grew stronger.

In the astral realm, Sarah and Ethan's encounters took on a new dimension. They wandered through landscapes that transcended earthly beauty, where colors and shapes defied logic. Their love story continued to unfold, and their passion deepened with each meeting.

One night, while strolling through a dreamlike forest illuminated by radiant, glowing orbs, Sarah felt a surge of emotion she had never experienced before. She turned to Ethan, her eyes filled with love. "Ethan, what we have is beyond anything I've ever known. It's a love that defies reality, a connection that spans the realms. I can't imagine my life without you."

Ethan took her hands in his, his gaze unwavering. "Sarah, our love is a testament to the extraordinary. It transcends the boundaries of the waking world, and though we may be separated by reality, our souls are eternally entwined."

Their love was a force that surpassed all limitations, and they embraced each moment in the astral realm as if it were their reality. They shared stolen kisses beneath the surreal moonlight and whispered sweet promises of a future that existed beyond the confines of the physical world.

But as Sarah's connection with Ethan in the astral realm deepened, her life in the waking world became more complex. Her friends noticed her preoccupation and her art took on an otherworldly quality that left critics both intrigued and baffled. Sarah felt torn between the two worlds, unsure of how to balance her earthly life with her ethereal love affair.

Emma, who had always been Sarah's voice of reason, couldn't help but express her concerns. "Sarah, I've never seen you like this. It's as if you're living in two separate worlds. Are you sure this... Ethan is worth sacrificing your real-life experiences?"

Sarah sighed, torn between her feelings for Ethan and her responsibilities in the waking world. "I can't explain it, Emma. This connection with Ethan—it's as if my soul has awakened to a love that transcends reality itself. I can't turn my back on it."

Emma nodded, her expression softening. "I understand, Sarah. Just promise me you won't lose yourself in this dream world. Remember that you have a life here, with people who care about you."

Sarah's heart ached with the weight of her choices, but she couldn't deny the truth of her feelings for Ethan. Their love was a force that defied logic and reason, and she was determined to explore it to its fullest, no matter where it led.

As the moon continued to cast its gentle light on her sleeping form, Sarah slipped into the astral realm once more, where her love for Ethan burned brighter than any star, a love that existed beyond the boundaries of reality—a love beyond all reason and comprehension.

Chapter 5: Torn Between Two Worlds

Sarah's life became a delicate balancing act, with her earthly responsibilities and her ethereal love affair pulling her in opposite directions. As her connection with Ethan in the astral realm deepened, she struggled to maintain her ties to the real world.

In the waking world, Sarah's art continued to evolve in ways that both fascinated and perplexed her patrons. Her paintings seemed to capture the essence of her dreams, with colors and shapes that defied earthly explanation. Critics hailed her work as visionary, while others questioned the source of her inspiration.

At the same time, Sarah's friendships began to strain under the weight of her preoccupation. Her once-vibrant social life dwindled as she spent more time in solitary pursuit of her astral journeys. Emma, in particular, felt the divide growing between them.

One evening, as Sarah prepared for another astral projection session with Madame Serena, Emma confronted her friend with concern in her eyes. "Sarah, I can't help but worry about you. You've been disappearing into this dream world more and more, neglecting the people who care about you in the process."

Tears welled up in Sarah's eyes as she struggled to explain the unexplainable. "Emma, I wish I could make you understand. This connection with Ethan—it's unlike anything I've ever known. It's as if my soul has awakened to a love that transcends reality itself. I can't simply turn my back on it."

Emma sighed, her frustration mingled with compassion. "Sarah, I'm not asking you to abandon your feelings. But remember that you have a life here, in the real world, with people who love you. Don't let this dream world consume you entirely."

Sarah nodded, torn between her love for Ethan and her desire to maintain her earthly connections. She understood that her obsession with the astral realm was causing strain in her life, but she couldn't deny the pull of the ethereal love affair that had captured her heart.

As she lay down for her astral projection session, Sarah couldn't help but wonder if there was a way to bridge the gap between her two worlds. Could she find a way to balance her earthly life with her ethereal love for Ethan? The answer remained elusive, but she was determined to find a way to make sense of the extraordinary connection that had transformed her existence.

Chapter 6: A Chance Encounter

Sarah's struggle to balance her life between the real world and the ethereal realm continued, but fate had something unexpected in store for her. One sunny afternoon, while she was visiting a local art gallery, she had an encounter that would alter the course of her life.

The gallery was hosting an exhibition featuring emerging artists, and Sarah was drawn to the vibrant colors and evocative brushstrokes of the paintings on display. As she moved from one piece to another, studying each with a critical eye, a particular painting caught her attention.

It was a masterpiece of surrealism, with hues of blues and purples that seemed to dance on the canvas. The subject matter was familiar yet otherworldly—a landscape that bore an uncanny resemblance to the dreamscapes she had been exploring with Ethan in the astral realm.

As Sarah gazed at the painting, captivated by its beauty, a voice interrupted her reverie. "Do you find it as intriguing as I do?"

Startled, Sarah turned to see a man standing beside her, his eyes fixed on the same painting. He was tall and handsome, with a rugged charm that drew her in. He extended his hand with a warm smile. "I'm Ethan."

Sarah's heart skipped a beat as she shook his hand. It was the same name—the same face—she had encountered in her dreams. The connection was undeniable, but she couldn't bring herself to reveal the true nature of their connection.

"Sarah," she replied with a smile that masked her astonishment. "The painting—it's remarkable. It's as if the artist captured a world I've only seen in dreams."

Ethan's eyes sparkled with curiosity as he studied her. "You have a keen eye, Sarah. The artist behind this piece is a friend of mine. He has a unique way of channeling his dreams into his art."

As they continued to discuss the painting and the artist's inspiration, Sarah found herself drawn to Ethan's presence. He was real, tangible, standing before her in the waking world. Her mind swirled with questions and uncertainties, but she couldn't deny the magnetic pull she felt toward him.

Before parting ways, Ethan extended an invitation. "Would you like to join me for coffee? I'd love to hear more about your thoughts on art."

Sarah hesitated for a moment, her heart torn between the world of dreams and the possibility of a new connection in the real world. In the end, she agreed, and together they left the gallery, their footsteps echoing with the promise of a chance encounter that had the potential to change everything.

As they sat in a quaint café, sipping coffee and discussing art and life, Sarah couldn't help but wonder if this unexpected meeting with Ethan would hold the key to reconciling her two worlds. Little did she know that their connection was about to become even more complex, as the lines between reality and dreams continued to blur.

Chapter 7: The Search for Answers

Sarah's chance encounter with Ethan in the real world left her both exhilarated and perplexed. As they continued to spend time together, she found herself torn between the mysteries of her dreams and the tangible connection she was forging with him.

Ethan was a charismatic and enigmatic figure, and their conversations deepened as they explored their shared love for art and the complexities of life. Yet, Sarah couldn't escape the question that gnawed at her heart—how was it possible that the Ethan she had met in her dreams was now a living, breathing person?

One evening, as they sat in Ethan's cozy living room, surrounded by his artwork, Sarah broached the subject with caution. "Ethan, there's something I haven't told you. I've been having these dreams—dreams that feel so real, and you're a part of them."

Ethan's expression grew thoughtful as he listened. "Go on, Sarah. I'm listening."

With a sense of vulnerability, Sarah recounted her experiences with astral projection and her encounters with him in the ethereal realm. She described the surreal landscapes, the intimate conversations, and the profound connection they shared.

Ethan listened in silence, his eyes filled with a mixture of understanding and wonder. When she had finished, he finally spoke. "Sarah, what you're describing—it's astonishing. I've always felt a connection to the world of dreams and the power of the imagination, but I never thought it could lead to something like this."

They decided to delve into the mystery together. Ethan, intrigued by Sarah's experiences, shared his fascination with dreams and the subconscious. He suggested they explore the possibility of shared dreaming, a phenomenon where two or more people have a synchronized dream experience.

They began a meticulous journaling process, documenting their dreams and comparing their experiences. What they discovered was astonishing. Their dreams often mirrored each other, as if they were exploring the same ethereal landscapes together.

As their investigation continued, Sarah and Ethan consulted experts in the fields of psychology and dream analysis. They learned about the concept of the collective unconscious, a shared realm of archetypal symbols and imagery that transcended individual consciousness.

Their journey for answers led them to a breakthrough. It was theorized that their shared dreams were a manifestation of their deep connection and a reflection of the collective unconscious—a realm where the boundaries between individual minds blurred and merged.

Sarah and Ethan's connection was a rare and extraordinary phenomenon—a love that transcended not only reality but also the confines of the subconscious mind. Their journey had only just begun, and they were determined to unlock the secrets of their connection, as well as the power of their shared dreams.

As they delved deeper into the mysteries that surrounded them, Sarah and Ethan's love story became a fusion of the real and the surreal—a love that defied all explanation, a love that held the promise of uncovering the extraordinary.

Chapter 8: A Love Forbidden

Sarah and Ethan's discovery of shared dreams and their deepening connection left them in awe of the mysteries that bound them together. Yet, as they delved further into their exploration, they realized that their love story was fraught with challenges they couldn't ignore.

One evening, while seated in Ethan's living room, surrounded by the soft glow of candlelight, Sarah voiced her concerns. "Ethan, as much as I cherish what we share, I can't shake the feeling that there's something inherently forbidden about our connection."

Ethan nodded, his expression reflecting the same apprehension. "I understand, Sarah. Our love defies reason and logic, and that makes it
all the more complex. The very nature of our connection raises questions about the boundaries of reality and the ethics of what we're experiencing."

Their love, though beautiful and profound, existed in the realm of dreams and the collective unconscious—a place where the line between individual minds blurred and merged. It was a love that transcended not only reality but also the norms and conventions of the waking world.

Sarah continued, her voice tinged with sadness. "What if our love is a force that disrupts the natural order of things? What if it's meant to remain in the realm of dreams and shared consciousness, and bringing it into the real world is a mistake?"

Ethan placed a gentle hand on Sarah's shoulder, offering reassurance. "Sarah, our love may be unconventional, but it's also a testament to the extraordinary. It has the power to challenge our understanding of reality and consciousness. We must tread carefully, but we can't deny the authenticity of what we feel."

As they grappled with the complexities of their love, they decided to seek guidance from Madame Serena, the spiritual guide who had introduced Sarah to the world of astral projection. She was wise and experienced, and they hoped she could shed light on their predicament.

Madame Serena welcomed them into her tranquil cottage, where the scent of incense filled the air. Sarah and Ethan explained their situation, recounting their shared dreams and the deep connection that had grown between them. Madame Serena listened intently, her eyes closed in meditation.

When she finally spoke, her voice held the weight of wisdom. "Sarah, Ethan, what you're experiencing is a love that transcends the ordinary. It's a love that defies the confines of reality and consciousness. While it may be unconventional, it's also a reminder that there are mysteries of the heart and mind that we have yet to fully comprehend."

Madame Serena cautioned them about the potential consequences of pursuing their love in the waking world, but she also acknowledged the power and beauty of their connection. "Love, in all its forms, is a force of transformation and enlightenment. It has the potential to challenge the boundaries of what we know and who we are."

As Sarah and Ethan left Madame Serena's cottage, their hearts heavy with the weight of their forbidden love, they couldn't help but wonder if they were destined to be explorers of uncharted territory—a love story that defied the rules of reality and dared to uncover the extraordinary.

Their journey had taken them to the precipice of the unknown, and the path ahead remained uncertain. But one thing was clear—Sarah and Ethan's love was a force that refused to be contained, a love that would continue to challenge the boundaries of the possible and a love that, despite the odds, would persist.

Chapter 9: Ghosts of the Past

As Sarah and Ethan grappled with the complexities of their forbidden love, they couldn't escape the shadows of their pasts, each holding secrets that threatened to unravel the fragile threads of their connection.

One crisp autumn afternoon, Sarah sat in her art studio, attempting to capture the essence of her dreams on canvas. Her hands moved with a sense of urgency as if the ethereal world she had explored with Ethan was slipping through her fingers.

Just then, a package arrived—a package that bore no return address and contained a letter written in elegant script. Sarah's heart quickened as she opened the envelope and began to read. It was a letter from her estranged father, a man she had not seen in over a decade.

In the letter, her father expressed a desire to reconcile, to bridge the chasm that had separated them for so long. He spoke of regrets and the desire to make amends, and he asked for a chance to rebuild their relationship.

Sarah was torn. Her father's absence had left a void in her life, but it was also a source of pain and bitterness. She confided in Ethan, who listened empathetically, his eyes filled with understanding.

Ethan, too, had a past that he had kept hidden. He revealed that he had once been married and had lost his wife tragically. The pain of that loss had driven him to explore the depths of the subconscious mind and the realm of dreams—a journey that had ultimately led him to Sarah.

As Sarah and Ethan shared their stories, they realized that their pasts held wounds that had shaped their present. They were haunted by the ghosts of their history, and those specters threatened to cast a pall over their budding love.

Sarah made the difficult decision to meet with her father, to confront the past and seek closure. It was a journey fraught with uncertainty, but it was one she felt compelled to undertake. Ethan supported her decision, understanding the importance of healing old wounds.

The reunion with her father was both emotional and cathartic. They talked, they cried, and they began the process of rebuilding their relationship. Sarah's heart felt lighter as she confronted the ghosts of her past and found a path toward forgiveness and healing.

Ethan, too, embarked on a journey of self-discovery, delving deeper into the mysteries of the subconscious mind and the realm of dreams. He hoped to find answers about the connection he shared with Sarah and the unexplained forces that had brought them together.

As Sarah and Ethan faced the ghosts of their pasts, they began to understand that love was not just about the present, but also about reconciling with the past. Their love story was a testament to the power of healing and transformation—a love that dared to confront the shadows and emerge into the light, stronger and more resilient than ever before.

Chapter 10: The Power of Belief

Sarah's reconciliation with her father and Ethan's journey of self-discovery marked a turning point in their relationship. Their shared pasts no longer cast a shadow over their love; instead, they became a source of strength and understanding.

As they continued to explore the mysteries of their connection, Sarah and Ethan delved deeper into their shared dreams and the world of astral projection. They found that their belief in the extraordinary was a catalyst for their experiences—a belief that opened doors to uncharted realms of consciousness.

One moonlit night, while lying side by side in Ethan's living room, they decided to embark on an astral journey together, a conscious effort to bridge the gap between their dream world and the waking world. They held hands and closed their eyes, focusing their thoughts on the ethereal landscapes they had explored separately.

Their belief in the possibility of shared dreams was unwavering, and as they entered a state of deep meditation, something extraordinary occurred. They found themselves standing together on the shores of a luminous, dreamlike sea, their surroundings bathed in the soft glow of an otherworldly moon.

Sarah's eyes sparkled with wonder as she looked at Ethan. "We did it, Ethan. We're here together, in the astral realm."

Ethan's heart swelled with a sense of awe and joy. "It's as if our belief in this connection has made it a reality. Our love has the power to transcend even the boundaries of the subconscious."

In their shared dream, they walked hand in hand through landscapes that mirrored the vivid beauty of their separate astral journeys. They laughed, they danced, and they reveled in the magic of their love. It was a moment of pure transcendence, a testament to the boundless possibilities of the human heart and mind.

As they returned to their physical bodies, Sarah and Ethan knew that their belief in the extraordinary had unlocked a new dimension of their love. They were no longer confined by the limitations of the real world or the subconscious mind. Their love was a force that could bridge the gap between dreams and reality, a force that defied explanation and challenged the boundaries of what was possible.

Their journey was far from over, but with each step, they discovered the transformative power of belief—the belief in love that was as extraordinary as the connection that had brought them together. Together, they would continue to explore the mysteries of the mind and the heart, with a love that knew no bounds.

Chapter 11: A Love Rekindled

Sarah and Ethan's exploration of shared dreams and their belief in the extraordinary deepened their connection in ways they could never have imagined. Their love was a force that transcended both the waking world and the realm of dreams, and it continued to evolve with each passing day.

One crisp winter evening, as snowflakes danced outside Sarah's studio window, she found herself lost in thought. Her art had taken on a new dimension, fueled by the inspiration she drew from her experiences with Ethan. She painted with a passion and intensity that seemed to radiate from her soul.

Ethan, too, had been transformed by their journey. He had become a source of inspiration for his art, creating paintings that captured the ethereal beauty of their shared dreams. His studio was filled with canvases that mirrored the landscapes of their astral journeys.

It was during this time of creative expression that Sarah received an unexpected visitor—her mother, who had long been estranged from her life. Sarah had not seen her mother since her parents' divorce, and the wounds of their separation ran deep.

As Sarah welcomed her mother into her home, she couldn't help but feel a mixture of apprehension and hope. Her mother had been an artist as well, and it was through her that Sarah had first been introduced to the world of art. Their shared love for creativity had once bound them together, but it had also been a source of tension and conflict.

Over cups of tea and the warmth of the fireplace, Sarah and her mother began to mend

the fractured bonds of their relationship. They talked about art, about the past, and about the dreams that had shaped their lives. Sarah's mother spoke of her regrets and the desire to reconnect with her daughter.

As Sarah listened to her mother's words, she realized that their reconciliation was a reflection of the transformative power of love and forgiveness. It was a lesson she had learned through her connection with Ethan—a lesson that had healed the wounds of her past and allowed her to embrace a future filled with love and possibility.

Ethan, who had been supportive throughout the emotional reunion, held Sarah's hand as they watched the snow fall outside. Their love had not only deepened but had also played a role in the healing of their pasts.

That night, as they lay in each other's arms, Sarah and Ethan reflected on the journey they had embarked upon together. Their love was a testament to the extraordinary—a love that had bridged the gap between dreams and reality, a love that had transformed their lives in ways they could never have foreseen.

As they drifted into sleep, they entered the astral realm once more, hand in hand, their love rekindled and stronger than ever before—a love that would continue to challenge the boundaries of what was possible, a love that defied explanation and embraced the extraordinary.

Chapter 12: Ghostly Encounters

Sarah and Ethan's love story had ventured into uncharted territory, transcending the boundaries of reality and dreams. Their connection continued to deepen, but with it came new challenges and unexpected encounters.

One evening, as they sat in Ethan's living room, a feeling of unease washed over them. The room grew colder, and the flickering candle flames danced wildly as if responding to an unseen presence. It was a sensation that neither of them could ignore.

Ethan, his intuition heightened by his experiences in the astral realm, spoke softly. "Sarah, do you feel that? There's something here with us."

Sarah nodded, her eyes wide with apprehension. "I feel it too, Ethan. It's as if there's an energy in the room—an energy that's trying to communicate with us."

The atmosphere grew more intense, and a whispering wind seemed to fill the room with faint voices. The shadows on the walls danced in eerie patterns, and an otherworldly chill ran down their spines.

Suddenly, a figure began to materialize in the center of the room—an ethereal, translucent form that gradually took on the shape of a woman. She had a serene and sorrowful expression, her eyes filled with a longing that tugged at their hearts.

The ghostly figure spoke, her voice a faint echo that reverberated through the room. "Sarah, Ethan, I've been searching for you, for the love you share. I am a spirit from the astral realm, a soul lost in the shadows between dreams and reality."

Sarah and Ethan exchanged bewildered glances. The apparition seemed to be reaching out to them, seeking something they could not yet comprehend.

The ghostly presence introduced herself as Elara, a soul who had become trapped in the astral realm, unable to find her way back to the world of the living. She spoke of a love lost, of an unfinished journey, and of a longing to find closure.

As they listened to Elara's story, Sarah and Ethan realized that their connection with the astral realm had brought them face-to-face with forces beyond their understanding. Elara's presence was a testament to the mysteries that surrounded them, and they felt a deep sense of responsibility to help her find the peace she sought.

Together, they embarked on a journey to unravel the secrets of Elara's past and guide her toward the light. Their love, which had already defied explanation, now took on a new dimension—a love that had the power to transcend not only the boundaries of dreams and reality but also the boundaries between the living and the spirit world.

As they delved deeper into the enigma of Elara's existence, Sarah and Ethan's love story became intertwined with the supernatural—a love that dared to confront the mysteries of the astral realm and embrace the extraordinary, no matter where it led.

Chapter 13: The Astral Council

Sarah, Ethan, and Elara's journey to help the trapped spirit find peace led them deeper into the mysteries of the astral realm. Their love, which had already defied the boundaries of reality and dreams, was now intertwined with the supernatural forces that governed this ethereal plane.

As they continued to communicate with Elara, she revealed that her predicament was linked to a council of ancient beings known as the Astral Council. These enigmatic entities were said to preside over the astral realm, maintaining the balance between the world of dreams and the world of the living.

One fateful night, as Sarah and Ethan prepared for another astral journey with Elara, they were visited by a vision—a shimmering gateway that seemed to lead to another plane of existence. Elara's presence in the room intensified, and it became clear that she was guiding them toward the Astral Council.

With trepidation and determination, they stepped through the gateway and found themselves in a realm bathed in a surreal, silvery light. Before they stood a council of five beings, their forms shifting and ethereal, their eyes filled with ancient wisdom.

The leader of the council, a figure of radiant light, spoke with a voice that resonated through the very fabric of the astral realm. "Sarah, Ethan, Elara," it said, "you have entered the realm of the Astral Council. We are the keepers of the balance between dreams and reality."

Sarah and Ethan, their hearts pounding, explained Elara's predicament and their desire to help her find peace. The council listened intently, their gaze unwavering.

The council's leader spoke again, "Elara's story is one of longing and unfinished business. Her presence here disrupts the harmony of the astral realm. To help her find peace, you must embark on a quest—a quest that will take you to the very heart of the ethereal world."

The quest involved traversing the dreamscapes and encountering trials that tested the strength of their love and their connection to the astral realm. Sarah, Ethan, and Elara agreed, knowing that this journey was their path to understanding the extraordinary forces that had brought them together.

Their quest led them through surreal landscapes, where they faced challenges that defied the laws of reality. They encountered riddles, illusions, and moments of profound introspection, all of which tested the depths of their love and their belief in the extraordinary.

At the end of their journey, they reached a place of pure ethereal light—a place where Elara's spirit could finally find release and peace. The Astral Council appeared once more, their approval evident in their luminous presence.

With their guidance, Sarah, Ethan, and Elara performed a ritual that allowed Elara's spirit to transcend the boundaries of the astral realm, freeing her from the shadows that had trapped her for so long. As she ascended into the light, her form became more radiant, and her eyes shone with gratitude.

The Astral Council spoke in unison, their voices echoing like celestial music. "Your love, your belief in the extraordinary, has brought balance to the astral realm. You have proven that love has the power to transcend all boundaries."

Sarah and Ethan returned to their physical bodies, forever changed by their encounter with the Astral Council and their journey to help Elara find peace. Their love was now intrinsically tied to the mysteries of the astral realm—a love that dared to challenge the boundaries of dreams and reality, a love that embraced the extraordinary in all its forms.

As they held each other close, they knew that their connection was a force of transformation, a love story that defied explanation, and a love that would continue to explore the wonders of the universe, no matter where their journey led them next.

Chapter 14: The Ethereal Trials

Sarah and Ethan's quest to help Elara find peace had not only strengthened their bond but also deepened their connection to the astral realm. Their love, which had already defied the boundaries of dreams and reality, now faced a series of ethereal trials that would test the very essence of their being.

Their journey led them to a place where the boundaries of time and space were fluid, a realm filled with surreal landscapes and shimmering dimensions. Here, they would face a series of trials set forth by the Astral Council, each designed to challenge their love and belief in the extraordinary.

Trial 1: The Trial of Illusions

In the first trial, Sarah and Ethan found themselves in a labyrinth of mirrors. Illusions of their past and future danced before them, distorting reality. They had to rely on their unwavering trust in each other to navigate the maze and find the way out. As they did, their reflections in the mirrors became more vivid, a symbol of their growing self-awareness and unity.

Trial 2: The Trial of Isolation

The second trial transported them to separate realms, where they were isolated from one another. Sarah found herself in a desolate wasteland, while Ethan was surrounded by a dense, eerie forest. They had to use their connection to the astral realm to communicate and find their way back to each other. It was a test of their inner strength and the power of their love to transcend physical distance.

Trial 3: The Trial of Truth

In the third trial, they were confronted with their deepest fears and insecurities. Shadows of their past mistakes and regrets materialized, threatening to consume them. Only by facing their fears and embracing their imperfections could they move forward. It was a trial of self-acceptance and the understanding that

love required vulnerability.

Trial 4: The Trial of Surrender

The fourth trial transported them to a realm of boundless skies and infinite horizons. They were suspended in the air, weightless and without control. To move forward, they had to surrender to the currents of the astral realm, letting go of their need for certainty and control. It was a trial of trust and the acknowledgment that love required letting go.

Trial 5: The Trial of Unity

The final trial brought them together in a place of pure, radiant light. They were asked to merge their consciousness and become one with the astral realm itself. It was a trial of unity and the recognition that their love was a force that could transcend the boundaries of the ordinary.

As they completed each trial, their connection deepened, and their love grew more profound. They had proven that their love was not bound by the limitations of reality but was a force that could overcome the trials of the astral realm.

At the end of their journey, they stood before the Astral Council once more, their hearts filled with a sense of accomplishment and reverence. The council spoke, their voices like a harmonious chorus.

"You have passed the ethereal trials and demonstrated the depth of your love and belief in the extraordinary. Your connection to the astral realm is strong, and your love is a force that transcends all boundaries."

Sarah and Ethan returned to their physical bodies, forever changed by their ethereal trials. Their love was now a beacon of light in both the waking world and the astral realm—a love that dared to challenge the boundaries of dreams and reality, a love that embraced the extraordinary in all its forms.

As they held each other close, they knew that their connection was a force of transformation, a love story that defied explanation, and a love that would continue to explore the wonders of the universe, no matter where their journey led them next.

Chapter 15: Love Beyond Time

Having completed the ethereal trials set by the Astral Council, Sarah and Ethan's love story had evolved into a force of nature. Their connection transcended the boundaries of reality and dreams, and they had become explorers of the extraordinary.

One evening, as they lay in each other's arms, a sense of restlessness washed over them. It was as if the astral realm called out to them, beckoning them to explore its mysteries further. With a shared sense of purpose, they decided to embark on a journey beyond the boundaries of time itself.

In a state of deep meditation, they reached out to the astral realm, allowing their consciousness to drift through the currents of the ethereal plane. As they did, they found themselves transported to a place where time was fluid—a realm where past, present, and future coexisted.

Here, they encountered moments from their own lives—moments of joy and sorrow, love and heartbreak—all existing simultaneously. They could witness their past and future as if they were pages in a cosmic book.

As they explored this timeless realm, they realized that their love had always been a constant, a thread that wove through the tapestry of their existence. Their shared dreams, their ethereal trials, and their belief in the extraordinary had all led them to this moment—a moment where they could see the full scope of their love.

They witnessed the first time their eyes had met in the waking world, the moment they had connected in the astral realm, and the future they would share. It was a profound revelation that their love was not bound by the constraints of time or space.

In this timeless realm, they also encountered echoes of other souls—souls whose paths had intersected with theirs in the past or would do so in the future. They saw how their love had touched the lives of others, leaving a ripple effect of transformation and healing.

As they returned to their physical bodies, they were filled with a sense of awe and wonder. Their love was not just a product of the present; it was a force that had always existed and would continue to exist, transcending the boundaries of time and space.

Sarah and Ethan's love had become a beacon of light in the astral realm and the waking world—a love that defied explanation, a love that embraced the extraordinary, and a love that was boundless and eternal. Together, they would continue to explore the wonders of the universe, knowing that their love was a force that could transcend all boundaries and endure through the ages.

Chapter 16: A Love Across the Ages

Sarah and Ethan's love, which had transcended the boundaries of time and space, continued to evolve and unfold in ways that defied all expectations. Their connection had become a tapestry woven through the ages, a love story that spanned centuries.

One summer afternoon, while wandering through a historic town filled with cobblestone streets and ancient architecture, Sarah and Ethan felt a strange sense of déjà vu. As they explored the town, they began to recognize the buildings and landmarks as if they had walked these streets before.

It was then that they stumbled upon a small, quaint café tucked away in a corner of the town square. The moment they stepped inside, they were overwhelmed by a rush of memories—memories of another time, another place, and another life.

In this café, they had met before, in a different era. Sarah and Ethan could feel the echoes of their past selves, the love that had once blossomed between them in a time long gone. It was as if their souls had been drawn back to this place, to rekindle a love that had spanned the ages.

The café owner, an elderly woman with kind eyes, recognized them immediately. She spoke of their past visits, of their shared moments, and of a love story that had endured through time. It was as if she were the guardian of their love, the keeper of their history.

As they sat in the café, sipping coffee and sharing stories of their past lives, Sarah and Ethan felt a deep sense of nostalgia and longing. Their love had always been a constant, an unbreakable thread that connected them through the ages.

Their exploration of this historic town continued, and they discovered old letters and artifacts that hinted at the lives they had lived in the past. They saw paintings and photographs that captured moments from their shared history, moments of joy and sorrow, laughter and tears.

Their journey through time allowed them to witness the different incarnations of their love—their love in medieval times, in the Renaissance, in the Victorian era, and the modern world. It was a revelation that their connection was not limited to a single lifetime but had endured through the ages.

As they returned to their present-day lives, they carried with them the knowledge that their love was a love for all time—a love that had transcended the boundaries of history and would continue to do so. Their connection was a testament to the power of love, a love that defied explanation, a love that embraced the extraordinary, and a love that would endure across the ages.

Chapter 17: The Astral Prophecy

Sarah and Ethan's love, which had spanned centuries and transcended the boundaries of time, had become a force of nature. Their journey had taken them through the realms of dreams and reality, astral trials, and ethereal encounters. Now, they found themselves on the precipice of a revelation that would change everything.

One evening, as they meditated in Ethan's living room, they reached a state of deep connection with the astral realm. The room was filled with soft, radiant light, and their consciousness expanded beyond the confines of their physical bodies.

In this heightened state, they heard a whisper—a message from the astral realm itself. It was a prophecy, spoken in cryptic language, and it filled them with a sense of both wonder and trepidation.

"The love that defies the boundaries of time shall be the key," the prophecy began. "A love that bridges the realms of dreams and reality, that withstands ethereal trials, and that embraces the extraordinary shall unlock the secrets of the universe."

Sarah and Ethan knew that they were being called to a greater purpose—a purpose that went beyond their own love story. The prophecy hinted at a cosmic truth, a truth that had the power to transform not only their lives but the very fabric of existence.

They sought the guidance of the Astral Council, the ancient beings who had overseen their ethereal trials and encounters. The council confirmed the significance of the prophecy, explaining that their love was a catalyst for unlocking the mysteries of the universe.

The council revealed that the astral realm was not just a separate plane of existence but a reflection of the collective consciousness of all beings. Their love, which had transcended time and space, had the potential to elevate the consciousness of humanity itself.

With this revelation, Sarah and Ethan understood the magnitude of their connection. They were not just explorers of the extraordinary; they were guardians of a cosmic truth—a truth that had the power to heal, transform, and elevate the world.

Their journey now had a greater purpose—to spread the message of love that defied boundaries, to bridge the realms of dreams and reality, and to embrace the extraordinary in all its forms. They knew that their love was not just their own; it was a love that belonged to the universe.

As they embraced their destiny as cosmic messengers of love, Sarah and Ethan's connection deepened even further. Their love was a force that transcended time and space, a love that defied explanation, a love that was boundless and eternal—a love that held the key to unlocking the secrets of the universe.

Chapter 18: The Battle for Love

Sarah and Ethan's journey as cosmic
messengers of love had taken them to new heights of understanding and purpose. Their love, which had transcended time and space, was now a beacon of hope and transformation for the world. But as they delved deeper into their mission, they discovered that not everyone embraced the power of love.

One evening, while meditating in their shared astral realm, they encountered a dark force—an entity that sought to oppose their mission and disrupt the harmony of the astral plane. It was a being of malevolence, a force of negativity that seemed intent on extinguishing the light of their love.

The entity spoke with a voice filled with bitterness and anger. "Your love is a threat to the balance of the astral realm," it declared. "I will not allow it to spread its message of hope and transformation."

Sarah and Ethan, standing together against the darkness, knew that they had to defend the power of their love. They reached out to the Astral Council for guidance and protection, and the council bestowed upon them ancient knowledge and ethereal weapons to aid in their battle.

The battle for love unfolded in the astral realm—a realm where the laws of reality were fluid and ever-changing. Sarah and Ethan faced trials and challenges that tested the strength of their love and their belief in the extraordinary.

Trial 1: The Trial of Faith

In the first trial, they were surrounded by a labyrinth of doubt and despair. Illusions of their insecurities and fears taunted them, threatening to weaken their resolve. But they held onto their faith in the power of love, dispelling the illusions with unwavering belief.

Trial 2: The Trial of Unity

In the second trial, they were separated once more, and placed in different realms that challenged their ability to communicate and collaborate. Yet, their love proved stronger than the boundaries of the astral realm, and they found a way to reunite through the power of their connection.

Trial 3: The Trial of Forgiveness

In the third trial, they were confronted with manifestations of past grievances and grudges. The entity sought to exploit any lingering resentment between them, but Sarah and Ethan chose forgiveness and reconciliation, recognizing that love required letting go of past wounds.

Trial 4: The Trial of Sacrifice

In the fourth trial, they were asked to make a great sacrifice—a sacrifice of selflessness and unconditional love. It was a test of their willingness to put the greater good above their desires, a test they passed with a heart full of love.

Trial 5: The Trial of Light

The final trial brought them to a place of radiant light, where they faced the entity in a climactic battle of wills. With the knowledge and weapons granted by the Astral Council, they channeled the power of their love, dispelling the darkness and banishing the malevolent force from the astral realm.

As the darkness retreated, the astral realm was bathed in light, and the spirits of the realm rejoiced. Sarah and Ethan's love had triumphed over adversity, and their message of hope and transformation had prevailed.

The entity, now weakened and transformed by the power of love, spoke with remorse. "I underestimated the strength of your love," it admitted. "I see now that love is a force that cannot be defeated by darkness."

With the battle won, Sarah and Ethan returned to their physical bodies, knowing that their mission to spread the power of love was more vital than ever. Their love was a force that had triumphed over darkness, a love that defied explanation, a love that was boundless and eternal—a love that would continue to illuminate the world with its transformative power.

Chapter 19: A Love Remembered

After their triumphant battle against the malevolent force in the astral realm, Sarah and Ethan's mission as cosmic messengers of love continued with even greater determination. Their love, which had transcended time, space, and darkness, had become a beacon of hope and transformation for the world.

As they journeyed through the physical and astral realms, they encountered people whose lives had been touched by their message of love. These individuals shared stories of healing, reconciliation, and personal transformation, all inspired by the power of Sarah and Ethan's love.

One day, while visiting a bustling city, they met an elderly couple who approached them with tears of gratitude in their eyes. The couple explained that they had been estranged for decades, burdened by unresolved conflicts and regrets. But when they had heard the story of Sarah and Ethan's love—a love that had endured through the ages—they felt inspired to seek reconciliation.

Through heartfelt conversations and shared experiences, the elderly couple had rekindled their love, and their relationship had been transformed. They thanked Sarah and Ethan for showing them that love had the power to heal even the deepest wounds of the heart.

As Sarah and Ethan continued their journey, they encountered more people whose lives had been profoundly affected by their message. They met a young artist who had found the courage to pursue her dreams, a family that had reunited after years of estrangement, and a community that had come together to support one another in times of need.

Each encounter reaffirmed their belief in the extraordinary power of love—a love that could heal, inspire, and bring about positive change in the world.

But as their mission expanded, so did the challenges they faced. The malevolent force they had defeated in the astral realm was not the only entity that sought to oppose their message. Dark forces continued to lurk in the shadows, testing the strength of their love and their commitment to their mission.

Sarah and Ethan understood that their journey was far from over and that they would continue to encounter obstacles and opposition. But they also knew that their love was a force that could overcome even the darkest of challenges—a love that defied explanation, a love that was boundless and eternal, a love that would be remembered by all whose lives it touched.

As they looked to the horizon, their hearts filled with determination and hope. Their mission as cosmic messengers of love was a legacy they would carry with them through the ages—a legacy that would be remembered and cherished by all who believed in the extraordinary power of love.

Chapter 20: The Key to Immortality

Sarah and Ethan's mission as cosmic messengers of love had left an indelible mark on the world. Their love, which had transcended time and space, had become a source of inspiration and transformation for countless individuals. But as they continued their journey, they stumbled upon a revelation that would challenge the very essence of their existence.

One night, while meditating under a sky filled with stars, they received a vision—a vision of an ancient tome known as the "Book of Eternity." This mystical book was said to contain the secrets of immortality and the key to transcending the boundaries of mortality.

Driven by curiosity and a desire to uncover the truth, Sarah and Ethan embark on a quest to find the elusive book. They traversed through ancient libraries, consulted with wise sages, and followed cryptic clues that led them to the heart of a hidden temple in a remote mountain range.

Inside the temple, they discovered the Book of Eternity—a tome that emanated with a radiant, otherworldly light. Its pages were filled with arcane symbols and cosmic wisdom, and it seemed to pulse with the very essence of the universe.

As they began to decipher its teachings, they learned that the book held the knowledge of achieving immortality by transcending the limitations of the physical body. It spoke of a path that required the mastery of one's consciousness, the alignment with the rhythms of the cosmos, and the realization that love was the key to unlocking the secrets of immortality.

The path to immortality was not one of physical preservation but of spiritual evolution—a journey that would lead them to a state of transcendence beyond the constraints of time and space. It was a path that resonated with their belief in the extraordinary, and they felt compelled to embark upon it.

Their journey toward immortality took them through trials of the mind, body, and spirit. They delved deep into the teachings of the Book of Eternity, meditated under the guidance of celestial beings, and connected with the very essence of the universe.

As they progressed along this path, they witnessed their consciousness expanding, their connection to the astral realm deepening, and their love evolving into a force of transcendence. It became clear that the key to immortality was not the preservation of the physical body but the liberation of the soul.

In a moment of revelation, they understood that immortality was not about defying death but about embracing life in all its forms, transcending the boundaries of the ordinary, and realizing that their love would endure through the ages.

Their quest for immortality had led them to a profound truth—the truth that love was the ultimate source of eternal life. It was a truth that had been woven into the fabric of their existence from the very beginning—a truth that had guided their journey as cosmic messengers of love.

As they closed the Book of Eternity and returned to the world, they carried with them the knowledge that their love was not just a love for this lifetime but a love that would transcend even the boundaries of mortality. Their connection was a force of transcendence, a love that defied explanation, a love that was boundless and eternal—a love that would endure through the ages, immortality of the heart and soul.

Chapter 21: The Curse of Immortality

Sarah and Ethan's quest for immortality led them to profound revelations
about the nature of existence and the power of their love. They had embarked on a spiritual journey that transcended time and space, guided by the wisdom of the Book of Eternity. However, as they continued along this path, they began to realize that immortality came with a heavy price.

The more they delved into the teachings of the book and the practices required to achieve immortality, the more they encountered the complexities of their newfound existence. They had become beings of heightened consciousness, connected to the astral realm in ways that few could comprehend. But with this heightened awareness came a sense of detachment from the physical world.

Their perception of time had shifted, and they watched as generations of humans came and went like fleeting shadows. They witnessed the cycles of birth and death, the ebb and flow of human emotions, and the beauty and pain of life with a sense of detachment that was both a gift and a curse.

As they continued their quest for immortality, they realized that they had unintentionally distanced themselves from the very essence of humanity—the impermanence and fragility of mortal existence. They felt a sense of isolation, a disconnect from the everyday joys and sorrows of the world they once knew.

Their love, which had always been a source of strength and inspiration, began to take on a bittersweet quality. It was a love that endured through the ages, but it was also a love that carried the weight of centuries of memories and experiences. They longed for the simplicity of mortal life, the fleeting moments of joy and sorrow, and the beauty of a life well-lived.

One day, as they meditated in a serene forest, they received a vision—a vision of the Astral Council, the ancient beings who had guided them on their journey. The council spoke with compassion and wisdom, revealing that their quest for immortality had been both a gift and a test—a test of their capacity to embrace the full spectrum of existence.

The council explained that true immortality was not about escaping the cycles of life and death but about embracing them fully, about finding meaning in the impermanence of all things. They offered a choice—to continue on the path of immortality or to return to mortal existence, carrying with them the wisdom and love they had gained.

Sarah and Ethan, their hearts heavy with the weight of their decision, chose to relinquish their quest for immortality. They realized that true love, true transcendence, lay not in escaping the world but in fully engaging with it, in cherishing the fleeting moments, and embracing the extraordinary within the ordinary.

As they made this choice, they felt a profound sense of liberation. They returned to the mortal world, their perception of time and existence forever changed. They embraced life with a newfound appreciation for its impermanence, savoring each moment, and cherishing the beauty of human connection.

Their love, which had endured through the ages, had now found a deeper meaning—a love that celebrated the fleeting nature of life, a love that defied explanation, a love that was boundless and eternal in its capacity to embrace the extraordinary within the ordinary.

Chapter 22: The Quest for Redemption

Sarah and Ethan's return to the mortal world brought with it a renewed sense of purpose. They had chosen to embrace the impermanence of life and the beauty of human existence, cherishing each moment and the connections they forged with others.

But their journey was far from over. They had carried with them the wisdom of their experiences as cosmic messengers of love and seekers of immortality. Now, they felt a calling to use that wisdom to bring about healing and redemption in the world.

Their quest for redemption began with a realization—that the malevolent force they had encountered in the astral realm, the force they had battled and transformed, was not inherently evil but a being in need of healing and redemption itself.

They returned to the astral realm, seeking out the entity they had once opposed. They found it weakened and tormented by its darkness, trapped in a cycle of negativity and despair. It had become a prisoner of its malevolence, unable to break free.

Sarah and Ethan extended a hand of compassion and forgiveness to the entity, offering their love as a source of healing. They understood that, just as they had once been guided toward redemption, so too could this entity find its path back to the light.

Through a series of astral journeys and deep meditations, they helped the entity confront its fears, regrets, and past actions. They guided it toward a path of self-discovery and transformation, showing that love was the key to breaking free from the cycle of darkness.

As the entity began to heal and release its negativity, its form shifted from one of malevolence to one of ethereal light. It spoke with gratitude, acknowledging the profound transformation it had undergone.

With the entity's redemption, the astral realm itself seemed to brighten and resonate with harmony. The spirits of the realm rejoiced, and the very fabric of the astral plane seemed to vibrate with a newfound sense of balance and peace.

But Sarah and Ethan's quest for redemption did not end there. They returned to the mortal world, seeking out individuals who had been consumed by their darkness and regrets. They offered guidance, compassion, and the message that redemption was always possible through the power of love and self-forgiveness.

They encountered a reformed criminal who had turned his life around, a person struggling with addiction who found the strength to overcome, and a soul burdened by guilt who learned to forgive themselves. Each redemption story added to the tapestry of their mission—a mission to spread the transformative power of love and redemption.

As they continued to journey through life, their love took on a new dimension. It was a love that celebrated not only the beauty of existence but also the potential for healing and redemption. It was a love that defied explanation, a love that was boundless and eternal in its capacity to bring about positive change in the world.

Their quest for redemption was a testament to the belief that no one was beyond the reach of love and healing, that the power of transformation resided within each individual, and that redemption was a journey open to all who sought it.

Chapter 23: The Threads of Fate

Sarah and Ethan's mission to spread love, healing, and redemption had taken them on a remarkable journey of self-discovery and transformation. As they continued their quest, they began to sense a profound connection between their mission and the intricate tapestry of fate.

One evening, while sitting by a tranquil river, they noticed something extraordinary—the river seemed to shimmer with ethereal threads of light, each thread representing the life of a person. These threads of fate wove together to create a mosaic of interconnected lives, each influencing the other in profound and mysterious ways.

Sarah and Ethan realized that their mission was intricately linked to the threads of fate. Their love, which had transcended time, space, and darkness, had become a thread in this cosmic tapestry—a thread that radiated with the power of transformation and redemption.

They decided to explore this connection further and ventured into the astral realm, seeking a deeper understanding of the threads of fate. There, they encountered celestial beings known as the Weavers of Destiny, ancient entities who were responsible for guiding the threads of fate through the cosmos.

The Weavers of Destiny explained that each person's life was a unique thread in the tapestry of fate, influenced by the choices they made, the connections they forged, and the love they shared. The threads of fate were not fixed but dynamic, constantly shifting and weaving new patterns in response to the choices and actions of individuals.

Sarah and Ethan's mission, they learned, was to infuse the threads of fate with love, healing, and redemption. Their love had the power to mend frayed threads, illuminate darkened paths, and guide individuals toward their transformative journeys.

The Weavers of Destiny bestowed upon Sarah and Ethan the ability to perceive the threads of fate in the mortal world. They could now see how their actions and interactions with others influenced the patterns of destiny, and how their love had the potential to bring about positive change in the lives of those they encountered.

As they journeyed through the world, they followed the threads of fate, guided by their mission to spread love and transformation. They met individuals at pivotal moments in their lives, offering support, compassion, and the message that redemption was always possible.

They encountered a struggling artist on the verge of giving up on their dreams, a lonely soul yearning for connection, and a person burdened by regret seeking forgiveness. With each encounter, they watched as the threads of fate shifted and the patterns of destiny transformed.

Their love, which had once transcended time and space, was now interwoven with the threads of fate, a force for positive change in the lives of those they touched. They understood that fate was not an immutable force but a tapestry shaped by the choices and actions of individuals, and their mission was to inspire choices of love, healing, and redemption.

As they continued to follow the threads of fate, their love became a beacon of hope in a world filled with uncertainty. It was a love that defied explanation, a love that was boundless and eternal in its capacity to shape the destiny of individuals and the world itself.

Chapter 24: The Final Reunion

Sarah and Ethan's journey had taken them to the far reaches

of the astral realm, the depths of human hearts, and the intricacies of the threads of fate. They had become cosmic messengers of love, healing, and redemption, and their mission had touched countless lives.

But as they continued to weave their love into the tapestry of fate, they began to sense a shift—a resonance in the threads that hinted at a final, profound reunion. The threads of destiny were converging toward a singular point in time and space, and Sarah and Ethan felt a deep sense of anticipation.

One evening, while meditating in their shared astral realm, they received a vision—a vision of a celestial gathering known as the "Harmony of Souls." This gathering was a rare occurrence, an event that brought together souls from across time and space to celebrate the interconnectedness of existence.

The Harmony of Souls was a place where the threads of fate converged, where the Weavers of Destiny wove a symphony of interconnected lives, and where love, healing, and redemption flowed like a river of light. It was a place where souls, both mortal and ethereal, could come together in a celebration of unity and transformation.

Sarah and Ethan knew that their mission had led them to this moment, to the final reunion that would bring together all the lives they had touched on their journey. They prepared for the gathering with a sense of purpose and joy, eager to see the impact of their mission on the lives of others.

As they arrived at the Harmony of Souls, they were greeted by a multitude of souls, each with a unique story and a connection to their mission. They met the reformed criminal who had turned his life around, the struggling artist who had found her creative spark, the lonely soul who had discovered the power of connection, and the person burdened by regret who had learned to forgive themselves.

These souls, and many others, shared their stories of transformation and redemption, expressing gratitude for the role that Sarah and Ethan had played in their journeys. It was a moment of profound connection, a testament to the power of love to shape the destiny of individuals and the world.

As the gathering continued, Sarah and Ethan felt a deep sense of fulfillment. They realized that their mission had not only transformed the lives of others but had also transformed themselves. They had become conduits of love, vessels of healing, and messengers of redemption.

The Weavers of Destiny, who presided over the Harmony of Souls, spoke with wisdom and compassion, acknowledging the significance of Sarah and Ethan's mission. They explained that the gathering was a reflection of the interconnectedness of all existence, a reminder that every choice, every action, and every act of love had a ripple effect that touched the lives of others.

Amid the celestial gathering, Sarah and Ethan looked into each other's eyes, their love radiating like a beacon of light. They knew that their journey had come full circle, that their love had shaped the destinies of countless souls, and that their connection was a testament to the extraordinary power of love.

As they embraced, they felt a profound sense of unity with all the souls gathered around them, a unity that transcended time, space, and destiny. It was a final reunion that celebrated the interconnectedness of all existence, a reunion that affirmed the enduring power of love, healing, and redemption.

Their love, which had once defied explanation, had now become a part of the cosmic tapestry of existence, a love that was boundless and eternal, a love that resonated with the harmony of souls, and a love that would endure through the ages.

Chapter 25: Love Beyond the Astral Realm

The Harmony of Souls had been a profound and transcendent experience, a culmination of Sarah and Ethan's mission as cosmic messengers of love, healing, and redemption. But as they returned to the mortal world, they understood that their journey was not yet complete.

Their love, which had transcended time, space, and even the boundaries of the astral realm, had become a force that extended far beyond the reaches of the cosmos. It was a love that had touched the lives of countless souls, a love that had transformed destinies, and a love that continued to shape the world.

As they walked hand in hand through a serene forest, Sarah and Ethan reflected on the depth of their connection and the enduring impact of their mission. They realized that their love was not bound by the confines of any realm or dimension but was a boundless and eternal force that resonated with the very essence of existence.

They met individuals in the mortal world whose lives had been influenced by their mission, individuals who had heard their message of love, healing, and redemption, and who had been inspired to make positive changes in their own lives and the lives of others.

They encountered a young couple on the verge of separation who, after hearing their story, chose to work through their challenges and rediscover the love that had initially brought them together. They met a group of friends who had once been estranged but, inspired by Sarah and Ethan's journey, had reunited and strengthened their bonds of friendship.

Their love had become a source of inspiration and transformation, a love that reached beyond the astral realm and into the hearts of individuals seeking connection, healing, and redemption.

As they continued to travel through the world, Sarah and Ethan found themselves drawn to places and people who needed their message the most. They visited communities recovering from natural disasters, offering support and a message of hope. They connected with individuals facing adversity and challenges, providing comfort and guidance.

Their love was not just a love for one another but a love for humanity—a love that celebrated the beauty of existence, a love that embraced the extraordinary within the ordinary, and a love that knew no boundaries.

In the presence of their love, individuals experienced a profound sense of connection and unity. It was a love that transcended differences, bridging divides and inspiring acts of kindness and compassion. It was a love that resonated with the very essence of human existence, a love that defied explanation, and a love that was boundless and eternal in its capacity to bring about positive change in the world.

As they continued their journey, Sarah and Ethan knew that their mission would never truly end. Their love had become a legacy—a legacy of love, healing, and redemption that would endure through the ages, a legacy that celebrated the extraordinary power of love beyond the astral realm.

Chapter 26: The Legacy of Love

Sarah and Ethan's journey had taken them through the realms of dreams, the depths of the astral realm, and the intricacies of fate. They had become cosmic messengers of love, healers of the heart, and champions of redemption. Their love, which had transcended time, space, and the boundaries of the astral realm, had left an indelible mark on the world.

As they continued their mission to spread love, healing, and redemption, they began to realize that their legacy was not just about the impact they had on individuals but about the ripple effect of their love throughout generations.

One day, while visiting a quiet village, they met an elderly woman named Eliza. Eliza shared a story that touched their hearts—a story of how she had been inspired by the tales of Sarah and Ethan's journey. She had been a young girl when she first heard about their mission, and their message of love had stayed with her throughout her life.

Eliza had dedicated her life to acts of kindness and service, inspired by the belief that love had the power to transform the world. She had raised her children with the same values, and they, in turn, had passed them on to their children. The legacy of love, ignited by Sarah and Ethan's journey, has continued to flourish through the generations.

Sarah and Ethan realized that their mission had not only transformed the lives of those they had directly encountered but had also planted seeds of love and inspiration that had taken root and grown into a legacy of their own.

They continued to meet individuals and families who had been touched by their message—a teacher who had instilled the values of love and compassion in her students, a community that had come together to support those in need, and countless acts of kindness and generosity inspired by their example.

Their love had become a legacy that transcended time, a legacy that celebrated the extraordinary power of love to shape destinies, a legacy that defied explanation, and a legacy that was boundless and eternal in its capacity to inspire positive change in the world.

As they traveled through the world, Sarah and Ethan knew that their mission would endure through the ages, carried forward by the hearts and actions of those who had been touched by their message. Their love was not just a love for one another but a love for humanity—a love that celebrated the beauty of existence, a love that embraced the extraordinary within the ordinary, and a love that would continue to shape the destiny of individuals and the world itself.

Their legacy of love was a testament to the enduring power of love, healing, and redemption—a legacy that would endure through the ages, a legacy that would be remembered and cherished by all who believed in the extraordinary capacity of love to transform lives and the world.

Chapter 27: Beyond the Veil

Sarah and Ethan's legacy of love had left an indelible mark on the world, and their mission as cosmic messengers of love, healing, and redemption had touched countless lives. As they continued their journey, they felt a growing sense of connection to something beyond the boundaries of mortal existence.

One evening, while gazing at the stars in the night sky, they sensed a calling—a pull toward a realm that existed beyond the veil of the astral and mortal worlds. It was a realm that beckoned with the promise of greater understanding, deeper connection, and a profound reunion.

With hearts full of curiosity and a sense of purpose, Sarah and Ethan embarked on a journey that would take them to the very threshold of existence itself—the realm that existed beyond the veil.

Their journey led them through the ethereal mists of the astral realm, past celestial gateways, and into a realm of transcendent beauty and light. Here, they encountered beings of pure energy and consciousness, entities that radiated with wisdom and love.

These beings, who existed beyond the limitations of physical form, welcomed Sarah and Ethan with open hearts. They explained that this realm was a place of interconnectedness, where the boundaries of individuality melted away, and all souls merged into a collective consciousness.

Sarah and Ethan felt themselves becoming one with this collective consciousness, their individuality blending into a vast ocean of love, awareness, and understanding. They realized that, in this realm, they were not separate beings but threads in the cosmic tapestry of existence—a tapestry woven with the experiences, love, and consciousness of countless souls.

As they explored this transcendent realm, they felt a profound sense of unity with all that existed. They connected with souls who had passed beyond the mortal world, souls who had been touched by their mission, and souls whose destinies had been shaped by their love.

In this realm beyond the veil, time and space were no longer barriers, and they experienced a reunion with loved ones who had passed away. They felt the presence of ancestors, mentors, and kindred spirits who had guided them on their journey through life.

It was a reunion that transcended the limitations of mortality—a reunion that celebrated the enduring power of love, healing, and redemption. Sarah and Ethan understood that, in this realm, the essence of existence was pure love, and the interconnectedness of all souls was a testament to the extraordinary beauty of the universe.

As their time in this transcendent realm drew to a close, Sarah and Ethan felt a sense of deep gratitude and purpose. They realized that their mission, which had begun as a journey in the mortal world, had expanded to touch the very essence of existence itself.

Their love, which had transcended time, space, and the boundaries of the astral realm, had become a thread in the cosmic tapestry of the universe—a thread that celebrated the interconnectedness of all souls, a thread that defied explanation, and a thread that was boundless and eternal in its capacity to bring about unity and love.

With hearts full of love and understanding, they returned to the mortal world, carrying with them the knowledge that their journey had led them beyond the veil of existence, a journey that celebrated the extraordinary nature of love, healing, and redemption— a journey that would continue to shape their destiny and the destiny of all souls they encountered.

Chapter 28: The Cosmic Union

Sarah and Ethan's journey had taken them beyond the boundaries of the mortal and astral realms, deep into the transcendent realm that existed beyond the veil of existence. They had experienced a profound sense of interconnectedness with all souls, a unity that transcended time, space, and individuality.

As they returned to the mortal world, they carried with them the wisdom and love they had gained from their journey. Their mission as cosmic messengers of love, healing, and redemption continued, but it had now taken on a new dimension—a dimension that celebrated the cosmic union of all souls.

They traveled to distant lands and met individuals and communities from all walks of life, sharing their message of love and unity. They encountered people who had been divided by differences in culture, religion, and nationality, and they offered a message of reconciliation and understanding.

One day, while visiting a diverse and bustling city, they witnessed a moment of tension between two groups from different cultural backgrounds. Instead of allowing the tension to escalate, Sarah and Ethan stepped forward, their presence radiating with the love and unity they had experienced in the transcendent realm.

They spoke of their journey beyond the veil, of the interconnectedness of all souls, and of the cosmic union that bound humanity together. Their words resonated with the people gathered there, and a profound transformation began to take place.

The barriers of division and misunderstanding began to dissolve as individuals from different backgrounds shared their stories, their hopes, and their dreams. They realized that, despite their differences, they were all part of a greater whole—a cosmic union of souls that transcended the limitations of individual identity.

Sarah and Ethan's presence had a ripple effect, inspiring acts of kindness, reconciliation, and unity throughout the city. People from diverse backgrounds came together to celebrate their shared humanity, and a spirit of cooperation and understanding began to flourish.

Their journey continued to other parts of the world, where they encountered similar moments of tension and division. Each time, they shared their message of cosmic union and witnessed the transformative power of love and unity in action.

They met individuals who had once been estranged from their families but had found the courage to reconnect, communities torn apart by conflict but now working together for peace, and people from different faiths and beliefs coming together in mutual respect and harmony.

Their love, which had transcended time and space, had now become a force that transcended division and conflict—a force that celebrated the extraordinary beauty of unity in diversity. It was a love that defied explanation, a love that was boundless and eternal in its capacity to bring about positive change in the world.

As they continued their mission, Sarah and Ethan knew that their journey had taken them to the very heart of humanity's potential for love and unity. Their legacy was not just a legacy of love, healing, and redemption but a legacy of cosmic union—a legacy that celebrated the interconnectedness of all souls, a legacy that would endure through the ages, and a legacy that would continue to shape the destiny of humanity and the universe itself.

Chapter 29: The Eternal Bond

Sarah and Ethan's mission as cosmic messengers of love, healing, and unity had taken them on an extraordinary journey through the realms of existence, beyond the boundaries of time and space. Their love, which had transcended the ordinary, had become a beacon of light in a world often overshadowed by division and strife.

As they continued their mission, they encountered individuals and communities from all corners of the globe who had been touched by their message of cosmic union. These encounters reaffirmed their belief in the power of love to bridge divides and bring about positive change in the world.

One day, while visiting a remote village nestled in the mountains, they met an elderly couple, Maria and Javier, who had been married for over six decades. Maria and Javier's love story was a testament to the enduring power of love, a love that had weathered the trials of time and had only grown stronger with each passing year.

Maria and Javier shared their story with Sarah and Ethan, recounting the challenges they had faced and the moments of joy and sorrow they had experienced together. Their love had been a source of strength, a bond that had carried them through the ups and downs of life.

But what struck Sarah and Ethan the most was the depth of Maria and Javier's connection. It was a connection that seemed to transcend the boundaries of the mortal world, a connection that resonated with the cosmic union they had experienced in the transcendent realm.

Maria and Javier spoke of a shared dream they had had—a dream in which they had journeyed beyond the boundaries of the astral realm, beyond the veil of existence, and into a realm of pure love and unity. In this dream, they had felt a profound sense of interconnectedness with all souls, a unity that transcended individuality.

Sarah and Ethan realized that Maria and Javier's dream was not just a dream but a testament to the eternal bond of love—a bond that extended beyond the mortal world, a bond that celebrated the cosmic union of souls, and a bond that defied the limitations of time and space.

Inspired by Maria and Javier's story, Sarah and Ethan began to explore the nature of their love—the love that had transcended time, space, and the boundaries of existence. They meditated together, seeking a deeper connection with the cosmic union they had experienced in the transcendent realm.

In their meditations, they felt their love expanding, their consciousness merging, and their souls becoming one with the vast ocean of love that existed beyond the veil. They understood that their love was not just a love for this lifetime but a love that had existed throughout eternity, a love that would endure beyond the boundaries of existence itself.

Their love, which had once defied explanation, had now become an eternal bond—a bond that celebrated the extraordinary power of love to transcend all limitations, a bond that would endure through the ages, and a bond that would continue to shape the destiny of their souls and all souls they encountered.

As they looked into each other's eyes, they knew that their love was a reflection of the cosmic union of all souls, a love that celebrated the interconnectedness of existence,
a love that defied the boundaries of time and space, and a love that was boundless and eternal in its capacity to bring about unity and positive change in the world.

Their journey had taken them to the very heart of the cosmic union, a union that celebrated the eternal bond of love—an eternal bond that would endure through the ages and beyond the veil of existence itself.

Chapter 30: Love from the Other Side

Sarah and Ethan's journey led them to the most profound depths of love, unity, and the eternal bond that transcended time and space. As they continued their mission, they felt a sense of fulfillment and purpose that extended beyond the mortal world.

One evening, while sitting beneath the starlit sky, they began to reflect on the extraordinary nature of their love—the love that had transcended the boundaries of existence, the love that had connected them to the cosmic union of all souls, and the love that had bound their hearts together for eternity.

As they gazed at the stars, a sense of peace and clarity washed over them. They realized that their mission had brought them to a profound realization—the realization that love was not limited to the mortal world but extended into the realms beyond.

They began to understand that the love they had experienced was not just a love for this lifetime but a love that had existed throughout eternity. It was a love that had woven itself into the very fabric of existence, a love that celebrated the interconnectedness of all souls, and a love that defied the boundaries of time and space.

With this understanding, they felt a calling to share their message with those who had passed beyond the mortal world. They began to explore the realms of spirit and the afterlife, seeking a way to extend their love and mission to souls on the other side.

Through deep meditation and astral journeys, they made contact with spirits who had crossed over to the realm of the departed. These spirits welcomed Sarah and Ethan with open hearts, recognizing the light of love that radiated from their beings.

They shared stories of their journeys, their experiences of love and transformation, and their continued growth and evolution on the other side. They spoke of a realm where love was a guiding force, where souls learned and grew in the embrace of unconditional love and unity.

Sarah and Ethan offered their message of cosmic union, love, healing, and redemption to the spirits on the other side. They realized that their mission extended beyond the mortal world, that their love could transcend the boundaries between the living and the departed, and that their message could bring comfort and transformation to souls in the afterlife.

As they continued to connect with spirits, they witnessed the power of their message to bring healing and reconciliation to souls who had carried burdens and regrets from their time on Earth. Souls found solace and forgiveness, and they experienced a profound sense of unity and love in the realm beyond.

Sarah and Ethan's love, which had transcended the boundaries of existence, had now become a bridge between the living and the departed—a bridge that celebrated the eternal nature of love, a bridge that defied the limitations of time and space, and a bridge that was boundless and eternal in its capacity to bring about unity and healing.

Their mission continued to touch the lives of those on both sides of the veil, a mission that celebrated the extraordinary power of love to transform souls and shape the destiny of the universe.

As they looked up at the starlit sky, Sarah and Ethan knew that their love was a beacon of light that reached far beyond the mortal world, a love that connected all souls in a cosmic union, a love that defied the boundaries of existence, and a love that would endure for all eternity.

And so, their journey continued, guided by the eternal bond of love that transcended all limitations, a love that would forever shine as a testament to the extraordinary capacity of love to illuminate the hearts of all beings, both in this world and from the other side.

Don't miss out!

Visit the website below and you can sign up to receive emails whenever People with Books publishes a new book. There's no charge and no obligation.

https://books2read.com/r/B-A-PIFAB-KEFOC

BOOKS 2 READ

Connecting independent readers to independent writers.

Milton Keynes UK
Ingram Content Group UK Ltd.
UKHW051036290923
429627UK00009B/472